The Chaos

Gill Arbuthnott

The Chaos Quest

Kelpies

Kelpies is an imprint of Floris Books

First published in Kelpies in 2004
Published in 2004 by Floris Books
Copyright © 2004 Gill Arbuthnott
Reprinted November 2004

Gill Arbuthnott has asserted her right under the
Copyright, Designs and Patents Act 1988
to be identified as the Author of this Work.

The publisher acknowledges a Lottery grant
from the Scottish Arts Council towards the
publication of this series.

British Library CIP Data available

ISBN 0–86315–459-X

Produced in Poland by Polskabook

For Ellen and Robert, the Guardians of Chaos

Many thanks to all at Floris Books, especially Gale and Katy, for expertise and TLC; to George Harris for finding just the right book; to Mark and Helen Ringland for technical support; and to Cattie and Ali Hall for txt trnsl8ion.

What is left when all the words have bled away?

Contents

1.	The Calling	9
2.	The Traveller at the Ford	19
3.	Family Life	25
4.	Tisian	33
5.	Erda	41
6.	The Right Time	51
7.	Falling	61
8.	Through the Door	71
9.	First Aid	79
10.	The Letter	87
11.	Into the Woods	95
12.	In the Underworld	105
13.	Responsibility	111
14.	Choices	121
15.	Rosslyn	129
16.	The Invitation	137
17.	The Hunt	147
18.	Consequences	155
19.	Dust Devils	165
20.	Siege	173
21.	The Stardreamer	181

1. The Calling

For what seemed like eternity she hung in the void between the stars, blown by the winds of time and space, fire sparking around her. In the space of a thought, stars were born and died, galaxies spun, huge clouds of stellar dust formed, toppled and reformed. She drifted on the currents of space, always edging imperceptibly closer to the tiny, insistent voices that called to her. An age passed for her in the time it took for a drop of water to fall from a leaf tip.

The voices caught at her now, a frail net of shining, unbreakable sound. She twisted this way and that, but could not escape it. It drew her inexorably towards a tiny world, that hung like a pearl against the endless velvet night.

Nearer and nearer she was pulled, struggling, until she hurtled down, fiery as a meteor, down into darkness and was extinguished.

In the Underworld, The Great Ones watched the sky. The lights that people sometimes called the Dancers flamed across the night, blue and green and finally, red.

"It is done," said the Queen of Darkness.

The lights — the Northern Lights — burned in Edinburgh too, even though it was May and much too late in the year. A great display, people said, so rare at any time of year, never mind now. A few of the old ones remembered the ancient stories that they foretold disaster, but no one believed such things nowadays, not here.

In the Wildwood, Morgan the Hunter stooped to drink from a stream. The endless woodland summer stretched off in all directions, seemingly limitless. Against it, still as he was, he could scarcely be seen: brown hair and tanned skin, eyes the colour of beech leaves, brown clothes, bow the colour of birch bark.

The sounds of the wood were all around, the rustlings and whispering of the trees, the calling of birds, water dripping from Morgan's hand, the drone of bees and small insects.

All sound ceased.

Morgan looked up sharply, hair pricking on the back of his neck. There was a moment of poised silence, as though the world held its breath and then chaos broke loose in the wood, birds exploding from the boughs, rabbits, mice and weasels running together in fear, the black deer of the deep wood bursting from the trees, eyes wide in terror. Morgan watched them run until they were lost to sight among the trees and the Wildwood quietened around him once more.

He half expected the Summons and it came almost immediately.

He stepped into the Empty Place between worlds and times and felt the presences gathered there already. Since they would not speak, he broke the silence.

"What has happened? All the creatures of the wood felt something. What was it?"

"The Stardreamer has been called down."

"The Stardreamer? I thought that was nothing more than a tale."

'*You should know the truth of tales, Morgan the Hunter.*'

He made no answer.

"The Stardreamer must be found and brought to the Heart of the Earth."

"But how? He cannot be commanded."

"No, but he can be persuaded, or tricked, or trapped."

"Tricked?"

"Yes. But first he must be found. You are a hunter. Use your skill to track him down."

Gordon Syme looked at the open suitcase on the bed, then at the towering pile of clothes beside it. The case would fit into the pile right enough, but it wasn't going to work the other way.

He sighed and started to cull the clothes. He was no good at packing, not enough practice probably. This was the first proper holiday he'd have had in, what, five years? And even now it was his sister in Spain who'd arranged the whole thing for him.

"Come and stay in May before the weather gets too hot," she'd said. "You can afford it now you don't have to pay rent on a flat. I'd enjoy the company, you and Joe can have a few rounds of golf and the kids would love having their favourite uncle around for a while."

She'd been very persuasive, but then he'd wanted to be persuaded. Now all he had to do was pack. He managed to shut the case at the third attempt and lugged it downstairs ready for an early start in the morning. His clubs were already there. He looked hard at them and took out his second-best putter and propped it against the wall beside the table in the hall. What was he thinking, taking two putters?

Before he went to bed he went round all the rooms, checking that windows were locked and everything was where it should be. He wasn't quite sure why he bothered. He'd got used to the weird way the house behaved. That was how he thought of it now, as a sort of living thing. Windows that he left locked when he went out would be open when he came in and objects seemed to wander between rooms. But the really strange thing was that far from finding this scary, it didn't even seem surprising. He knew this was nothing to do with ghosts or poltergeists; it was something to do with time and with John Flowerdew, who had left him, albeit temporarily, this house.

Then there were the visitors. People turned up on his doorstep every so often, calling him by name, explaining that they had known John Flowerdew. They'd stay for a few hours, or a night, then leave. Or sometimes they wouldn't leave, they'd just be...gone. At first, he used to look for them, convinced they must be in the house somewhere, but even the strangest things could become routine and now he didn't bother. He just let them in, like it had said he was to do in Mr Flowerdew's will.

It was nearly six weeks since he'd last had one of these visits and even longer since he'd seen Kate and David. Kate and David who had played such a vital part in the impossible events that had taken place eighteen months ago ...

At first they'd come round often, as all three of them tried to come to terms with what had happened, but the visits had tailed off as real, ordinary life had taken hold of them again. They had keys to the house; that too had been specified in the will, not that their parents knew. "A place of refuge," the old man had called it in the instructions 'whenever one should become necessary.'

Occasionally he would come in and find one or other of them in the kitchen, or more likely in the old man's study, staring into space, thinking.

He'd hardly known them when the battle with the

Lords of Chaos had taken place that autumn, but after going through that, there were bonds between them that no one else could ever understand.

Kate seemed to have come through it fine, but he found himself worrying, sometimes, about David. He'd made such a sacrifice for them to win. Gordon doubted that he could have done as well if he had been put to the test. Although most of the time David acted as though everything was fine, he had periods when melancholy gripped him and it was then that Gordon would find him huddled in one of the big chairs in the study under the eaves. He'd learned that it was best to leave him alone to deal with it — even Kate couldn't lift these moods from him. He was marked by what had happened, what he'd done.

Gordon roused himself from his reverie and locked the back door, then made himself a cup of coffee and went up to bed to read about Spanish golf courses.

David Fairbairn was walking with his mother in Princes Street Gardens, eating ice cream, while around them snow fell, soft and quiet as feathers. It was warm and they had taken off their shoes to cool their feet in the snow that was already lying.

"I've got a Geography test tomorrow," he said to her, "and I don't know the work."

She smiled. "Don't worry, the answers are all in your teeth."

He nodded. Of course, he should have realized that himself. They strolled on, watching the children in the playground, then his mother looked up at the sky and stood as though she was listening and the ice cream dropped, un-noticed, from her hand. She looked back at David, her expression a mixture of fear and wonder.

"You must go now, she is coming."

He woke up.

He lay quite still for a moment, trying to fall asleep and find his way back inside the dream. There had been a time of course when he'd dreamed of his mother every night — at least, it was easier to deal with if he thought of it as dreaming — but such dreams were infrequent now and he always hated it when one ended.

That had been a strange one. It had all made sense while he was asleep, of course, the ice cream and snow and the bare feet, but the last things his mother had said had seemed out of place, not part of that dream at all.

You must go now, she is coming.

Who?

Kate Dalgliesh's dreams that night were haunted by howling. She tossed in her sleep, her dreams fragmented, but though she could never see them, the cold and lonely voices of the wolves always pursued her. The night seemed to last an age, and she woke bad tempered and unrefreshed.

Why the wolves again? Why now? Surely all that had died with Mr Flowerdew?

She woke in darkness, suddenly, surrounded by the smell of the crushed leaves and stems she lay on. For a long time, she lay quite still, absorbing the sensations of the leaves against her bare skin and of the movements her body made as she breathed — both quite new to her. Eventually a different sensation, unpleasant this time, replaced that of touch.

Cold, said the words in her head. She waited for the feeling to go, but instead it got stronger. She tried curling up tightly and for a little time, that helped, but the cold would not leave her alone.

Shelter, said the words and now she understood. Shelter. Find shelter away from the cold.

She rolled over and got up. There was a shape of yellow light against the darkness a little way off.

Shelter.

She made for it on uncertain feet.

The house put words into her head. *Door*, it said as it closed out the world of cold and leaves and dark. She stood inside the door listening to the quiet breath of the walls and waiting for the words to settle themselves in her head. They flew at her from all around, whirling about her in confusing patterns that gradually resolved themselves into a kind of order and she knew that she stood in a kitchen — a place for preparing food — and that she needed food, but not yet; first she needed warmth... clothes.

She wandered slowly through the rooms on the ground floor, picking things up and putting them down again, knowledge of the house seeping into her. There was nothing that served her purpose on the ground floor, so she went upstairs.

It was dark up here and she put a hand out to the wall to help feel her way. Her fingers brushed something and suddenly there was light blossoming above her. She stared fascinated, then looked away, half-blinded, to see what her hands had touched and pressed it again. The light disappeared.

Press. Light.

Press. Dark.

PressPressPressPress. LightDarkLightDark. Delighted, she played with it for a minute before moving on to open a door.

A small room with shiny walls and silver-shiny metal and white tubs. *Bathroom*, said the house. She waited to understand.

Aaah... She twisted a piece of metal and water poured from it. She cupped her hands and drank, then moved around the room sniffing things, feeling them.

She saw herself in the mirror, but did not yet understand that it was her. She moved her head from side to side and so did the being in the mirror. She reached out a hand and placed it flat to the glass and so did the other, but they did not touch. She turned back to the water to drink again, but now it was hot, puffs of cloudy vapour billowing up. She listened to the words in her head for a moment, then found the thing to stop the water going away and climbed into the tub and watched it fill around her. In the hot water she blossomed like a flower, the tightness of bracing herself against the cold floating out into the vapour around her. She slid down under the water as the bath overflowed.

Kate turned her key in the lock. "Hello! Anyone home?"

"Be a surprise if there is," said David, behind her.

As they had expected, there was no answer and they shut the door behind them, gathering up letters from the hall floor.

"Doesn't look like there's anything very interesting," said Kate as they examined the envelopes. Gordon seemed to lead a very dull postal life.

"What would you do if there was?" asked David.

"Dunno. Steam it open? That's what they do in books."

David shook his head. "Doesn't work. I tried it once. Wanted to see my school report before Dad did, but all that happened was that the ink ran and I had to pretend I'd dropped it in a puddle."

Kate grinned. "You never told me that before."

"Well, I felt really stupid when it didn't work. I think they must use different glue now."

"What?"

"On envelopes. It's always in old books that they steam them open. It probably only works on old envelopes."

Kate put the letters down on the hall table and wandered off to the kitchen in search of a jug of water for the plants — their official reason for being here — and a biscuit for herself.

The room was a mess, a box of cereal spilled on the big wooden table, with a carton of milk standing open beside it.

"He must have slept in and had to leave in a hurry," remarked David as he sniffed the milk and poured it down the sink, grimacing. Kate cleared up the cereal and found the biscuit tin, then they each filled a jug with water and began to check the plants. Although it was only a day and a half since Gordon had left, lots of the pots were dry and it took them nearly fifteen minutes to see to all the downstairs plants.

Upstairs there was more evidence of Gordon's hasty departure: a light left on and a tumble of clothes on the floor of his bedroom.

"He *really* must have been in a hurry," said David, "You know how neat he usually is."

The biggest mess awaited them in the bathroom, when they went in to get water for the upstairs plants. The floor was awash with water, the bath still full. The water in it was muddy, shreds of leaves and twig floating on the surface.

They looked at each other.

"Gordon wouldn't leave things like this, would he?" said Kate.

David shook his head. "It looks more like the house has had a visitor."

"Mmmn... I don't think they're still here though, do you?" asked Kate.

"No. It doesn't feel as though there's anyone here but us."

All the same, they checked all the other rooms, but there were no further signs of disturbance. They tidied up the bathroom and finished watering the plants.

As they were leaving David said, "I wonder if Gordon knew someone was coming?"

"Well," said Kate, "even if he didn't, if the house let someone in, they must be okay, don't you think?"

"Yes, I suppose so."

They locked the door behind them.

2. *The Traveller at the Ford*

Morgan was lost in his own thoughts as he made his way back to the village. He had no idea that people greeted him as usual as he passed their doors, much less that he answered them with reasonable coherence. It wasn't until he closed the door of his own house behind him and Thomas looked up sharply from the table where he was working that he became conscious of his surroundings again.

Thomas was Morgan's brother, five years the younger. They didn't look alike at all, apart from the colour of their eyes. Thomas was a couple of inches shorter and more lightly built, with hair the colour of a crow's wing and fine-boned good looks that had all the girls of the village trailing after him like a flock of sheep.

"Morgan? What's wrong?" He got up from the litter of wood shavings in front of him, putting down a knife, and came towards him. "Are you ill? You look terrible."

Morgan shook his head slowly. "I'm fine, just tired." He walked to the table and sat down heavily and pretended to look carefully at what Thomas had been doing, to avoid having to speak of what was troubling him.

"What does it do?"

"It catches a stick. This one." Thomas picked up a spill of wood fine as a bird bone. "It's a dog."

"I can see it's a dog. It's beautiful."

The thing that Thomas had been working on for hours lay on the table: a tiny jointed model of a sheepdog, strung together with waxed thread, beside it the beginnings of the stand that would conceal the threads and springs and levers that brought it to life.

"Who's it for?"

"Nicolas."

"He's only six. He'll pull too hard and break it."

Thomas shrugged. "His father asked me to make it for his birthday. It might last long enough to show his friends before he ruins it."

Morgan shook his head, smiling. Thomas looked at him more closely. "What has happened, Morgan? I felt something this morning. All the birds stopped singing. Is it something ... did they call you?"

Morgan nodded. "They have called the Stardreamer," he said flatly.

"But the Stardreamer is only a legend."

"No, he is real. And I have been set to find him and bring him to the Heart of the Earth by the Guardians. I cannot believe they have taken this risk. If the Stardreamer's power is released outside the Heart of the Earth then all the barriers of time and space will be destroyed and the Lords of Chaos will triumph utterly."

"He has that much power?" breathed Thomas.

"Enough to destroy the Worlds and everything in them. But perhaps he will have forgotten."

"What do you mean?"

"In whatever world he is, he will have taken physical form, but he will be ... empty ... at first, not knowing what he truly is or what he can do. That is the time when I must reach him and somehow persuade him to step into the Heart of the Earth and dream the Worlds safe." He passed a hand over his eyes. "I should pack. I set out at first light tomorrow."

"Let me come."

Morgan shook his head. "Thomas, you know this is not for you …"

"I've come with you before to search for people they want. Why not this time?"

"Can you not see? This time is different. The being I am searching for could destroy us all with the flick of a finger. Our mother did not leave you to my care for me to lead you into danger like this."

Thomas' expression hardened. "It is many years since she left me to be cared for by you. I am a grown man, in case you had forgotten. I make my own choices."

"You cannot help with this. You do not have the skills. Or the parentage," Morgan added, his face darkening.

Thomas flinched as though he had been struck.

"I'm going to pack. Goodnight." Morgan pushed past him out of the room, leaving him there, hands balled into fists at his side, face pale.

For a long while Morgan lay awake, thinking of what had just passed downstairs. From his unshuttered window at the top of the house he could see a small slice of sky. It was a clear night and he watched the first early-burning stars as he wondered what he should have done or said.

He'd always known there was something different about him. The first thing he became properly aware of was that he could find places in the Wildwood that no one else could. Not just hidey-holes for children's games, but real places that no one else seemed aware of: the secret glades where the black deer ran and the wild grey horses watched him without fear or curiosity as he stumbled about, amazed; the great thicket of briars, thick as one of his arms, with narrow paths between them leading to a still pool, no bigger than a cartwheel, which reflected not the sky above it, but some other place entirely.

Then, one day when he was ten and searching for a fledgling linnet to tame as a song bird, he wandered, unknowingly, into the Empty Place. He was so terrified by what he saw there that when he stumbled home that night he was speechless with fear and his mother looked into his eyes with a terrible foreboding and held him tight in his bed until he stopped shaking and fell asleep.

The next morning, she told him who he was.

"This village has been here in the Wildwood for hundreds of years," she began, "and in all that time it has been a safe place. No raiders have come here, nor floods, plague, nor forest fire. There are rituals that take place year after year to keep us in such safety: bargains made with the Gods. One of them is the ritual of the Traveller at the Ford.

"Each year all the men and women of the village draw lots; the one who is chosen spends the first night of harvest full moon in that little hut near the river bank, down by the ford.

"Some years it means no more than an uncomfortable night, but if someone should cross the ford between sunset and sunrise the person in the hut must do whatever is asked of them, however trivial, however terrible, to safeguard the village. There are all sorts of tales of what folk have done in the past to protect us.

"Eleven years ago, my name was drawn and I went to the hut by the ford. Such a long night it was; I lay there sleepless, watching the moon cross the sky, listening to the river, waiting for the sound of someone approaching. There was only a little time left before dawn when I heard the sound of a horse crossing the ford and a few seconds later the Traveller came into the hut ..."

She paused, her mind somewhere far off. "I never spoke of it to anyone until this day."

She gathered her thoughts. "For a year and a day I travelled with him, always thinking of home. Then he brought me back to the ford, with you just a babe."

She stopped talking, this time for so long that he thought she'd finished, and so started to rise from his chair. The movement seemed to bring her back from wherever she had been.

Then she told him who his father was.

Morgan woke the next morning dull-headed and unrefreshed, his mind still snagged on the odd images that had disturbed his dreams: a cave, glittering with fire, a little meadow of parched grass on top of a hill, and the face of a young woman with dark red hair and eyes the colour of copper coins.

The images stayed with him as he put what he needed into his pack and he was still brooding over them as he went downstairs.

In the half-light of the kitchen, Thomas sat waiting for him, booted feet on the table, pack on the floor beside him. Morgan groaned.

"I told you ..."

Thomas shrugged. "You can knock me senseless, bind me hand and foot and lock me in the barn, then have me follow you as soon as I get out if you want, but it would be simpler if we just went together, you know."

Turning his face to the wall, Morgan knocked his head against it a few times, just for the relief of the physical pain it brought. He was about to speak when Thomas said, in a quite different voice, "Mother didn't just tell you to look after me, you know. She worried about you. She knew you would have to face such difficult things. 'Don't let him lose his way in all of it, Thomas,' she said. 'Keep him safe.'"

"You never told me that before."

"I was saving it for when I needed it," replied Thomas, swinging his legs down from the table. "It's time we went, surely?"

Morgan sighed. "Come on then, but you'll have to keep up; I'm not waiting for you."

3. Family Life

She wandered through the streets, soaking up impressions, information, *words*. Words flew at her from all around, some making sense gradually, but most no more than patterns of noise and silence.

People stared at her, their eyes moving from her head to the ground. She stared back, curious and when she did so, most of them would avert their gazes. Not the small ones though, the children. They kept looking and smiled, or did not smile.

After a while she realized that she was the only one whose feet were not covered and that this, as much as anything else, was what made them stare.

Shoes.

That was what she needed. Shoes. Later she wandered back to the house that had taken her in. After a while she found some shoes there and put them on. They were much too large and her feet slipped around in them. She took them off again and put them by the door to wear when she went outside again, so that people would look at her face and not her feet.

She pulled off the clothes she wore, filled the big tub with water and lay in it for a long time, thinking. Her mind was beginning to put the words together to make sense. She had listened to others talking in the street and imitated it in her head as she walked. Now, lying in the steaming water, she practised talking.

"When's the next bus due?"

"Have you got any change, love?"

"Ha ha ha. Look at her."

"I'll meet you at eight o'clock."

"No you can't have any sweeties. You'll ruin your teeth."

Maybe when she next went out she would try speaking to someone.

David lay on his bed, his headphones on and his eyes shut, oblivious to the outside world, singing tunelessly at the top of his voice. It wasn't until there was a tap on his shoulder and he opened his eyes that he realized his father was in the room, trying to talk to him. He pulled the phones off and Alastair recoiled.

"Good grief, what volume's that at? You'll fry your brain. Who is it, anyway?" David opened his mouth to reply, but his father cut him off with a gesture. "No, don't bother telling me. I don't suppose it'll mean anything anyway.

"Tea's ready. Christine's been calling."

"Sorry. I didn't hear."

"You amaze me. Wash your hands before you come through."

"Okay."

When Alastair had left the room he lay back down and put the phones on again, but after a minute he thought better of it and got up to go and wash his hands. There was no point having another argument. It just got too tiring.

His dad and Christine were sitting at the table waiting for him when he went into the kitchen.

"Sorry."

"It's okay, David," said Christine soothingly, in the patient, reasonable voice that set his teeth on edge. She served out the food and they began to eat.

"This is delicious, Christine, isn't it, David?"

"Yeah, it's all right."

"That's a bit grudging, isn't it?"

"Leave it, Alastair," said Christine quietly, putting a hand on his arm.

"It's delicious, it's wonderful, it's the best food I've ever eaten," said David, his voice rising, "Can I just eat it now?"

There wasn't much conversation after that.

He didn't mean it to be like this. He knew she was trying and in fact, if he thought about it, there was nothing about her he actually disliked, she was pretty nice really. It was just seeing her sitting at the table with Dad, or in the sitting room where the big portrait that Mr Flowerdew had done of him, Dad and Mum hung over the mantelpiece that always upset him, no matter how hard he tried.

She wasn't Mum, but now that she was married to Dad he was confused. Where did that leave Mum now? Had Dad stopped loving her? Was he meant to forget about her, meant not to speak about her?

He didn't understand how things were supposed to work anymore. When it had been just Dad and him, they'd got used to it and looked after each other and had each tried, without saying anything, to fill the gap that Mum's death had left for the other. Then Dad had met Christine and everything had turned upside down. That wasn't quite true; he'd worked beside her for a long time and they'd always been friendly, but about a year ago they'd started going out on proper dates and it was nearly three months now since they'd got married.

He was pleased for Dad, really he was. They'd talked about it before Dad had asked her and David had felt okay about it then, but now that it was real and she was here in the house with them every night it was so different from what he'd thought, and he couldn't stop feeling that it was disloyal to Mum.

If only he could still talk to her the way he had done

when he had dreamed about the Lightning King. Maybe she could have told him that it was all right, told him what to do, how to behave with Christine. But he couldn't speak to her and whatever he did seemed to be wrong.

He'd talked to Kate about it, of course, and she'd listened and tucked her hair behind her ears as she always did when she was thinking hard, but she hadn't come up with the magic answer that a small, unrealistic part of him was hoping for.

Instead she had said, "I think you'll just both have to be patient with each other until you work out how you can…" She wrinkled her nose, looking for the right words, "… fit together without rubbing. I know that sounds stupid, but I can't work out another way to say it."

He knew she was right, but it didn't make it easier to do.

Back in his room he put the headphones back on and turned the volume up.

Kate groaned and chucked her pencil across the room in frustration. She'd tried and tried and she still couldn't get it to come out right. Maths homework. Terrible stuff and it seemed to get harder every week. She just couldn't get her mind round it at all. Muttering, she rolled over and reached for her phone to text Sarah to see if she knew what to do, but before she could, it bleeped and there was a message from David.

phone me now. can I cum over n help with hwork?
got 2 get out.

She sighed. That could only mean there had been another row between David and Alastair. She felt sorry for David: anyone would have some trouble accepting a step-mother, but for David, who'd had to lose his mum twice, it must be much worse. Even so, she couldn't help feeling (disloyally, she told herself) that David was being a bit unfair on Christine and Alastair.

She climbed down from her bunk and went through to the sitting room where her mum was listening to Ben's reading homework.

"Mum, can I ask David to come over and help with my maths homework? I don't understand how to do it."

"Surely you should be asking your teacher about it then, not David."

"C'mon Mum, please. He's good at explaining it. I won't just get the answers off him, honestly."

"No one's listening to me!" shouted Ben "and Floppy's in trouble!"

"Sorry Ben," said Mum. "Just hold on a second. Go on then Kate, but I want you to talk to your teacher about this too."

"Okay, okay, I will. Thanks."

She fled back to her room before she too was forced to listen to Ben tell her about Floppy.

David arrived twenty minutes later, still fuming and threw himself on the bed.

"I could move out when I'm sixteen if I had enough money, you know. How could I get the money?"

Kate let him rant in peace for a few minutes before she spoke.

"What was it about this time?"

"Nothing. As usual." He sat up. "Thanks for calling. What am I meant to be helping you with?"

"Maths, but you really have to. I can't do it. I was just going to call Sarah when I got your message."

David rolled his eyes to show what he thought of that solution. "What is it? Let's see." He read the questions and grinned. "Yeah. We did this a couple of weeks ago. It's okay once you get the hang of it, but it takes a bit of practice."

Kate decided, not for the first time, that it was very useful to have a best friend who was in the top maths set. For her, maths was a sort of soup of confusion, with the few bits and pieces she understood sticking above the surface like bits of bread.

After half an hour, she got it, sort of. Enough to have a reasonable go at the homework, anyway.

"Do you want to go round to Gordon's for a bit after school tomorrow?" she asked as she worked through it again.

"Yeah, all right. The plants probably need some water anyway. It's been quite hot."

Thomas hadn't spoken much since they left the house, an unusual situation for which Morgan was grateful, for his mind was in a whirl as it was.

However he thought of it, this search seemed madness. To have brought the Stardreamer to the Worlds was a terrible risk; he couldn't decide whether finding him or not finding him would be worse. He had no idea who he was looking for, but in his heart was an unshakeable conviction that he would know immediately if he found him. How to explain any of this to Thomas, or even what to try to explain …

If he was honest with himself however, he was glad to have Thomas at his side now as they made their way deep into the Wildwood, through the chorus of early morning birdsong, dew wetting their clothes as they walked along the narrow path.

They each carried a light pack. In addition, Morgan

had his bow and a long hunting knife, but Thomas
would never carry weapons. He had never been inter-
ested in hunting. When they went into the wood as
boys, Morgan would always emerge with a rabbit or a
pigeon he had brought down with a sling or bow, but
Thomas would come out with some piece of wood that
he wanted to carve. True to form, the only blade he
carried now was the little knife he used to make his
figures.

"So," said Thomas, breaking the silence, "where are
we going exactly?"

"I have no idea."

Thomas stopped walking.

"But he's in the Wildwood somewhere?"

"I don't know. I don't think so. I think I would ...
feel his presence."

"So," said Thomas, walking on, "where are we going?"

"To see Tisian."

They walked for nearly two hours before a wisp of
smoke told that they were near their goal. Ten minutes
more and they were standing in front of Tisian's home.

It didn't look like something you could rightly call a
house. It appeared to have grown rather than been
built, pushing its way out of the ground and into the
steep slope behind it, a living tree forming one of its
corner posts. Smoke rose from a jutting structure that
was presumably a chimney. The door stood ajar, sagging slightly on its hinges.

"So lads, what brings you to Tisian the Sorceress
today?" said a voice from inside and Tisian stepped
through the door, smiling.

4. Tisian

Tisian was tall enough to look Thomas in the eye and she did so now, laughing as she glanced into his open face, but growing still as she studied Morgan's expression.

As usual, she wore a dress of chaotic colour, patched with madder and umber, ochre and beech-leaf green. Her greying brown hair was twisted into an untidy knot at the back of her head, secured with a couple of goose quills already trimmed for writing. Thomas noticed that one of them had ink on the tip.

They had asked her years ago, when they were still boys, why people called her a sorceress. She had laughed, as she so often did and said, "Because I'm a woman who lives alone in the middle of the Wildwood. There are lots of folk think there must be something strange about me just because of that."

If she did have any sorcery it was of the same type as Morgan's: a gift for finding, ... people or places or things.

They sat with her now on the little patch of open ground in front of her ramshackle house, eating bread and honey and drinking the heather beer she had made for as long as they had known her.

When they had finished they sat in silence for a while, listening to the sounds of the wood around them.

"So, why have you come to visit? There's a reason, isn't there, Morgan? Who are you searching for?"

"A Stardreamer."

Her brown eyes opened wide. "I hope you don't really mean that."

He nodded and told her what he could.

"Of course! I felt it — the whole Wildwood felt it — when he fell into the Worlds." She shivered. "Do you have any idea where he is now?"

Morgan shook his head. "I don't have any sense of his presence in the Wildwood. I came to ask if you did."

"No. After that moment ... it was as though the whole world had shouted ... nothing. I fear the Stardreamer has gone elsewhere."

"That is as I thought. I came to make sure before I started opening the Doors needlessly."

"Morgan, what will you do if you find the Stardreamer?"

"I don't know. There's no way I can overpower him; he could kill us all as easily as beetles. Perhaps I can persuade him or trick him?

"That's why I brought Thomas," he added, trying unsuccessfully to lighten the gloomy mood, which had descended since the Stardreamer was first mentioned.

"You shouldn't have," she said abruptly, her face deadly serious.

"I made him," said Thomas. "He didn't ask me."

"What do you mean?" asked Morgan, ignoring Thomas and staring at Tisian's troubled face.

"Nothing," she said, with an unconvincing smile. "I'm getting to be an old woman; I want my lads safe where I can find them."

Their eyes locked. "I should send him back."

"He wouldn't go."

Thomas stood up. "I *am* here you know. Stop discussing me as though I'm a pet dog. Tisian's right: you know I won't go back Morgan, not unless you do."

There seemed nothing more to say. They left soon afterwards and set off to open a Door between the Worlds.

It hadn't been a bad day at school, thought Kate. The maths homework had been good enough to satisfy Mr Leslie and she'd had double Design and Technology, her favourite subject. This term she was making a display case for her sports trophies and it was turning out well. She had seen David in Geography and they had arranged to meet outside the school gate at the end of the day.

He was late.

He arrived a few minutes afterwards, out of breath, books spilling from his arms.

"Look at that," he said, gesturing at what had been his back pack. "It just tore open and everything fell out. What a mess."

One whole seam had given way. David stuffed it in the top of a litter bin. "Dad'll go mental. I've only had it three weeks."

Kate pulled it out of the bin again. "It can't be your fault. There must have been something wrong with it. Take it home and show your dad and he can take it back to the shop."

David looked at her with admiration. "That's brilliant! Why didn't I think of that? You know, for someone who can't do dead-easy maths you're quite clever."

She stuck her tongue out at him, then they got the escaped books under control and walked towards Mr Flowerdew's house, which they now tried hard to think of as Gordon's.

They bought crisps on the way and dawdled down the hill, eating and chatting.

"I heard a good joke today," said David.

"Go on then."

"What do you call an exploding monkey?"

"I don't know."

"A Ba-Boom!"

Kate grimaced. "Oh, that's so bad."

Now that they were at secondary school and in different classes for a lot of things, they didn't get so much time to talk as they used to. They still understood each other better than anybody else though. That would never change.

The gate still creaked when they pushed it open, just as it had the first time they visited the house, such a long time ago it seemed now.

They went under the rowan tree and opened the front door. Just inside lay a pair of Gordon's work shoes.

"That's funny," said Kate. "He can't have come back early, can he?"

They called his name, but there was no answer.

"Oh well, you know what this place is like," said David. "I'll put them back in his bedroom."

Kate went into the sitting room to choose a video. Mr Flowerdew had had a fantastic collection. They'd thought it was strange that he had a widescreen television at his age, but now she understood why he'd wanted it. They watched all sorts of things when they came here — sometimes in French or German or Japanese with subtitles which was great fun for half an hour, but usually got boring after that.

"Kate." David was there behind her suddenly, breathless.

"What is it?"

"Come and see — in Gordon's room — quiet."

They crept up the stairs to the first floor and went into the big bedroom. There, curled up on the bed like an animal, in a sort of nest of duvet, was a girl, maybe eighteen or nineteen. She had long, unkempt hair, dark, dark red and it looked as though the clothes she was wearing belonged to Gordon. The jeans were much too big and Kate was sure she recognized the horrible diamond-patterned sweater as one of Gordon's golf ones.

Speechless, they watched her for several moments, but, sound asleep, she didn't move. Finally they crept out and went downstairs again to the sitting room.

"Who do you think she is? Do you think she's broken in?"

"No," said Kate with conviction. "I'm sure no one can get into this house unless the house decides to let them in."

"But who can she be — and how come she's wearing Gordon's clothes?"

"I don't know."

There was something nagging at Kate: a feeling that she should know who the girl was, that she'd seen her, but the memory, if it really was one, eluded her for now.

"What do you think we should do?" she said uncertainly. "Wake her? Leave before she wakes? We can't just pretend she's not here."

"Well ... if the house has let her in she must be okay, but we can't just wake her. Imagine what a fright you'd get if two total strangers poked you awake."

"Maybe she's used to it if she goes around sleeping in other people's beds."

They thought for a moment.

"Let's put a video on like we were going to. Maybe the noise will wake her."

"And coffee. We'll make coffee. The smell might help."

Kate got up and turned to go through into the kitchen and gave a squeak of surprise. In the doorway to the sitting room stood the girl.

The three of them regarded each other in silence for

a few seconds that seemed to last much longer, then Kate found her voice.

"Hello. I'm sorry if we woke you. We didn't know anyone was here. Gordon's away and we came in to water the plants, I'm Kate by the way and this is David."

The girl hadn't moved. She stared silently at them.

"Do you understand? Do you speak English? You *can* speak, can't you?" asked David, to no avail.

"I'm Kate and this is David. What's your name?"

Nothing.

"You must have a name."

Nothing.

"Who are you?"

Who are you who are you who are you ... A sudden wind shook the branches of the rowan tree. A word unwound itself from deep within the Worlds and coiled upwards like a snake into her mind.

"I ... am ... Erda."

Her voice sounded as though it hadn't been used for a long time, like the sound of dry leaves rubbing against each other before they fall.

"Erda?"

"I am Erda." Stronger this time. She moved at last, turned and went towards the kitchen.

David and Kate glanced quickly at each other and followed.

In the kitchen, Erda opened cupboard doors seemingly at random until she found a box of cereal and began eating it in handfuls. She sat down on the floor with her legs crossed, concentrating on the food and nothing else.

When it became obvious she wasn't going to speak, David did.

"Have you been staying in the house?"

Erda looked up, frowning and seemed to think for a long time before she answered.

"I come for food ... and sleep ... and bath."

"So you know Gordon?" asked Kate.

Erda looked at her blankly. "No."

"How long have you been here?" Kate went on as Erda shoved another handful of cereal into her mouth.

She shrugged and there was another long pause before she answered. "I woke there." She pointed towards the back garden. "It was cold. I came inside. I found the food and the bath and these." She gestured at her clothes. It was the longest speech she had ever made, in all the aeons.

"But before you woke up in the garden ..." puzzled David, "where are you *from*?"

Erda said nothing. She raised her hand without hesitation and pointed out of the window to the leaden sky.

5. Erda

"D'you think she's mad?" asked Kate as they set off up the hill, having left Erda watching a video of something French.

"Well, she's definitely not normal, is she?"

"No. Maybe she's been in an accident and lost her memory or something."

"Mmmn ... maybe. Erda — what sort of name's that? I've never heard it before, have you?"

"No. Erda ... Erda. I don't know, maybe it's Norwegian or Swedish or something."

"Do you reckon it's safe to leave her here?"

"Well, we can hardly chuck her out on the street can we? Anyway, the house wants her there."

"But what if she *has* had an accident? Her family could be going mental looking for her and all the time she's camped out in Gordon's house eating cornflakes. Maybe we should tell the police."

Kate stopped suddenly and caught David by the arm. "That's it!"

"Okay. I wasn't sure, but ..."

"No, I don't mean that. We've seen her before David! It was nagging at me all the time back there: I was sure I recognized her and I've just remembered." She stopped and shook her head, a puzzled expression on her face. "But how can it be?" she said, almost to herself. "It doesn't make sense."

"*What*?" David almost yelled in exasperation. "*What* doesn't make sense? Where have you seen her?"

"We both have. The day of the Earth Tremor."

The Earth Tremor: a warning from the Lords of Chaos that time was coming apart; that they were

winning their age-long battle with the Guardians of
Time. But they'd stopped them. He and Kate and
Gordon and Mr Flowerdew. For a moment he was back
on the loch's edge, holding the sword, looking into his
mother's face for the last time.

"David?"

He shook his head. "Sorry. I was just trying to
remember ... Carry on."

"The day of the Earth Tremor. We'd been doing the
cake stall at the school fair and we went to buy a news-
paper, and the newsagent was pushing a girl out of the
shop ... I thought she was homeless ..."

"It was Erda," he breathed.

"Yes. I remember the sweater. It's so horrible. But
how could she have been wearing it then? Gordon didn't
even own it. Remember he showed it to us, said he got it
from an auntie for Christmas."

"That's right. Erda said she found the clothes in the
house, so it must be the same one, but how could she
have been wearing it a year and a half ago?"

They had reached the crossing at the top of the hill.
Kate hit the button and waited for the signal to change
to green.

"She's not someone normal who's had an accident
and lost her memory. She can move through time."

They walked in silence across the Links, avoiding
footballs and bikes.

"Who is she? *What* is she?" wondered David. "The
Guardians can't move through time, can they?"

Kate shook her head and tucked her hair behind her
ears. "Mr Flowerdew never made it sound as if they
could anyway."

"And she couldn't be one of the Lords of Chaos. He
— Mr Flowerdew — said they were ..." he searched his
memory for the right word "... *confined* or something

and couldn't get into the real world unless everything fell apart."

"We'd have noticed that, don't you think? Anyway, I'm sure she's not one of them. We've both met them. Erda *feels* different from them, you know?"

"Yes. So how does she do it and what is she?"

"I don't know."

After they had left Tisian's house and her worried expression behind, the brothers went deeper into the forest, to reach one of the secret places Morgan had found in his youth, so that he could open one of the Doors between the Worlds. He was troubled by what had taken place. He had known Tisian all his life and had never seen her frightened, but today, she had been. He had asked Thomas again to go back, but Thomas, predictably, had laughed at him.

An hour after noon they stopped to rest and eat, sitting side by side against a fallen trunk, legs stretched out in front of them. Morgan sat dozing, trying to push away the pain behind his eyes that had oppressed him all day. His brother's voice brought him awake.

"Morgan? I know that we have a rule that we never talk about who *you* are ..." His eyes flew open and his body tensed. "... but we have never once talked about who *I* am."

Morgan looked at him, taken aback. "What do you mean?"

"I can see some of what you see; I can pass through the Doors with you. Did you never wonder why?"

Morgan began to speak, but Thomas held up a hand and went on, "I know we have different fathers. I know who mine is as well as you know yours. I am the son of my mother's husband, but somehow in me flows a little of the blood that makes you what you are." Morgan flinched visibly. "You know how long the ritual of the Traveller at the Ford has protected our people. It seems likely to me that our great-great something grandmother took part in it and bore a child like you and from that child the blood has passed down and down the generations, un-noticed mostly, until what you could do made me realize what I could do."

Morgan was still silent.

"Why is it so difficult for you to accept that my destiny as well as yours may lie in this search?"

"I want to protect you."

Thomas turned to look Morgan in the face. "You can't. I don't need your protection. I can protect myself."

"How?" shouted Morgan, getting angrily to his feet. "All you'll carry is that stupid little wood-carving knife. How can you protect yourself with that?"

Thomas's voice was cool and measured. "You don't really think that your bow can protect us from the Stardreamer, do you? He'll shatter it like kindling if he wants to. That sort of protection is useless to us now."

Morgan turned away, his hands over his face, trying to quell the beats of pain in his skull. After a moment he spoke, measuring his words carefully.

"I'm sorry. I know you're right. I may as well have left my weapons in the house for all the good they'll do us." He found that Thomas had risen and come to put an arm across his shoulders, but went on anyway. "It's not destiny I fear. It's doom."

Soon afterwards they reached the place where the Door was hidden.

The glade was a silent place, always. No bird sang there, no insect hummed. Even the wind seemed to avoid disturbing its dangerous quiet. This was the place into which Morgan had blundered as a boy, before he realized what he was. Even now, for a moment he felt again the fear and awe he'd felt as a child of ten.

Briars rose in front of them, scores of years old, thick as a man's wrist, impenetrably fanged with thorns, the dark green leaves and blood-red blooms utterly still, though elsewhere in the Wildwood, a breeze was blowing.

They waited for the path to show itself and when it did they made their way quietly through the palisade of roses. Even Thomas's spirit was quenched in this place and he suppressed a shiver as he felt the hair rise on the back of his neck.

The still pool at the centre of the maze of tightly curving paths was as black as the pupil of a great eye. As they watched, they saw faint points of light sprinkled here and there in unfamiliar patterns. The pool reflected another sky to the one above them and wherever it was, it was night.

"Ready?"

Thomas nodded. They clasped each other's hands tightly and stepped into the black water ...

... and were on a treeless hillside under cold stars, scattered flakes of snow blowing in on the wind from the east.

They let their eyes adjust to the new darkness. Behind them the hillside rose in a sheer rock face for twenty or thirty feet, gashed by a narrow cave mouth, which was barely visible in the faint light of a half moon, the Door's location in this world. They gazed out into the grey and black distance and saw, here and there, the flicker and glow of fires, but no single place that seemed bright enough for a town or village.

Thomas shivered and wrapped his cloak tighter

against the chill. Beside him Morgan stood heedless of the cold, staring at the dark landscape as though he could illuminate it by force of will alone.

"Morgan?"

"Do you feel it?" Morgan raised his head like a hound scenting prey. "He is here. Somewhere out there. Not close, but perhaps beside one of these fires. Do you feel it?"

Thomas concentrated hard. All he felt was cold. "No, I can't feel anything." He let the silence grow for a minute. "What do you want to do?"

"We can't do anything until morning."

With these words Morgan roused himself from the half-trance he had been in and they settled themselves as far into the cave mouth as they could without finding themselves back in the briar glade again, and huddled into their cloaks against the cold to wait for daylight.

Morgan woke in a grey dawn, a thin layer of snow sifted over his cloak. Nearby, Thomas was a grey-white hummock against the darker grey of the rock.

As he came fully awake he became aware that something was different. He jumped to his feet, stumbled a few steps down the hillside, seeking this way and that.

"No!"

"Morgan, what is it? What's wrong?"

"He's gone. He's not down there any more. But ..." Morgan shook his head as though trying to dislodge a fly, "I can't explain it; he's here but he's not here. I knew he wasn't anywhere in the Wildwood, but this is different. It's as if he's here and not here at the same time."

"You're not making much sense, you know."

"Oh, I know all right. I don't make sense to myself."

Thomas got to his feet and walked a little way down the hill. "So what do we do now? Do you want to go down there and see what you can find out about him? Someone must know something about where he's gone."

"That's it!"

"Come on then."

"No, I don't mean that. He's not here, but he is here. It makes sense. He's not here, but he's here in some other time. We just need to open the Door in the right time." He turned and strode back to the cave mouth. "Come on. We have to go back to the briar glade and wait for the pool to change."

"We brought you some clean clothes," said Kate, a little nervously. "We thought you might like a change and I think these will fit you better."

Kate pulled underwear and socks, an old pair of jeans and a tee-shirt of her mother's out of her bag. David had a sweatshirt and a pair of trainers he didn't think Christine would miss.

Erda looked at the clothes as they held them out to her.

"For me?"

"Yes."

She took them without another word and stood waiting to see what would happen next.

"We brought some food as well. We thought we'd make you a meal. You could go and change while we do it," said Kate.

"Change?" Erda frowned. "How?"

"Change your clothes. Take the old ones off and put the new ones on," David explained.

Erda nodded and wandered off with the clothes.

Kate and David exchanged glances but didn't talk

until they were sure she was upstairs and out of earshot.

"She's weird," said David, putting ice cream in the freezer. It's like she's never seen anything before, doesn't understand anything.'

Kate pulled pizzas out of their boxes and set the oven temperature.

"I know what you mean, but I don't think she's stupid."

"No, neither do I, though I don't know why. It's as if she's seeing everything for the first time; as though she's from another planet or something."

Kate giggled. "Now *you're* being stupid. I mean, she isn't green, so she can't be."

David lobbed a tea towel at her head.

"Ha ha."

He turned round to find Erda in the doorway, watching them silently, a trainer in each hand. He wondered how long she'd been there. She didn't look angry or upset, so maybe she hadn't heard them talking about her.

"I don't understand these." She held up the trainers.

"Sit down and I'll show you," said Kate and proceeded to teach her how to tie a shoelace. Erda watched once, then did it perfectly.

"Good," said Kate, smiling.

"Good," said Erda and smiled back.

"Where are you from, Erda?" asked David.

She put her head to one side as though she was listening.

"I don't know. Everywhere."

Kate tried another tack. "How long have you been here?"

"Since I woke up in the garden."

"A few days?"

"A few days."

Kate wasn't sure if it was an answer or if Erda was just repeating her words.

"It's just that we thought we remembered seeing you once before, but it was eighteen months ago and you weren't here then, were you?"

"I wasn't here then."

Kate bent to look in the oven. The pizza was nearly ready. She and David busied themselves with plates and cutlery for a minute, Erda watching them curiously.

"I saw you out there," she said suddenly. Kate looked up. "When the man pushed me outside. You were both there."

6. The Right Time

Five times now they had stepped into the pool and emerged from the cave to find day or night or twilight; a ruined chapel and a city spread before them, or bare hillside and the distant flickering fires, and each time it had been only seconds before Morgan muttered, "No. He's here, but not now."

For two days they had waited as the sky in the little pool changed and changed again, venturing out into the Wildwood to rest or eat, for it seemed impossible to do either in the briar glade.

Morgan prodded the sleeping Thomas with the toe of his boot and got to his feet. "It's a while since we looked. We ought to check." Thomas nodded, not properly awake, and followed him yawning.

The sky in the pool was the washed, clear blue that comes after rain, wisps of white cloud trailing across it like tattered banners.

Thomas looked at Morgan expectantly. He sighed. "I don't know. Maybe it'll be different if we go through. I can't tell from here."

They clasped hands and stepped …

… through, into a morning that smelled of spring and green things growing. Thomas looked around and saw a chapel on the slope in front of them, not ruined this time, but whole, and recently built by the look of it.

"Well, it's a different …" he began, turning to speak to Morgan, stopping as he saw his face.

"He's here. *Now*. We've found the right time."

Thomas let a slow breath out. "Can you tell where?"

"That way." Morgan pointed immediately to the

walled town that clustered along a spur of rock a mile or two away. At the far end a castle dominated the highest point. Streets sloped away from it down the rocky spine to another large building, a church or monastery, near the bottom of the hill on which they stood. Between the hill and the monastery lay a loch, silver-blue in the morning light. "Somewhere in the town maybe."

"So now we ..."

"... go and find him and bring him back through the Door and take him to the Empty Place or the Heart of the Earth."

"And if he doesn't want to come?"

But Morgan was already walking towards the town and didn't answer.

Erda, Kate and David had become quite used to each other now and one or both of them managed to visit the house on most days, finding some excuse or other for their families. That part wasn't difficult: there were so many after-school clubs and friends they could be visiting that it never occurred to their parents to wonder at these absences, which were, in any case, seldom very long.

Erda's speech was becoming more fluent and she no longer seemed such a strange creature as she had at first. Not just because they'd become used to her either; it was as though she absorbed facts from her surroundings, plucked knowledge straight from people's brains.

She looked less odd now, dressed in clothes that Kate and David had managed to find that more or less fitted her. Kate had also persuaded her to comb her hair so that she looked less as though she'd blown in with the last high wind.

That was another weird thing, Kate thought, for as soon as she'd explained it, Erda was able to draw the comb smoothly down the length of her waving, dark red hair as though it had last been combed moments before. *Or as though she'd told it to unt ...*

Don't be stupid, Kate thought. As if anyone, however odd, could think their hair out of tangles.

Still ...

She and David had been so taken aback when Erda had said she remembered seeing them before that they hadn't really pursued it at the time. Now, as she sat teaching Erda to play snap, she brought the subject up again.

"Remember when you said you'd seen us when the man pushed you out of that shop?"

"Yes." Erda put down a seven.

"How long ago was that?"

Erda waited until Kate put down the Jack of Hearts before she answered.

"I don't remember." Three. "Last week sometime."

Eight.

"Soon after you came to the garden?"

Eight.

"Snap!" Erda picked up the cards and added them to her pile. "Two days after, I think. I don't remember well."

Kate was running out of cards. She put down the Queen of Diamonds.

"To David and me, it was much longer ago."

Erda looked at her, head tilted to one side.

"Maybe," she said finally, putting down a two.

"What do you mean?"

"Sometimes, when I go out, it is different."

Kate put a four on the pile.

"Different how?"

"Different words, different clothes. Different houses."

Kate's heart thudded heavily against her ribcage.

"Different ... time?" she asked slowly.

Erda tilted her head and thought again.

"Don't know. Time..." She thought about the word while she put down a ten. "I don't understand time. The words are not in my head to know it yet. But maybe ... maybe I come out in different times."

Kate put down her last card. Ace of Clubs.

"I win," said Erda happily.

After Kate had gone, Erda made a sandwich with jam and bread and raisins and went over what she and Kate had said in her mind as she enjoyed the sweet tastes.

She decided to go out in search of words that would tell her about time. She finished the sandwich, pulled on her shoes and tied the special strings.

As she did so she was aware of something new. It pulled at her, urging her to go out of the house. Since it was what she wanted to do anyway, she let it tug her towards and through the front door.

Outside lay a bright morning that smelled of spring and green things growing. In front of her, where the street usually was, lay a grassy slope and off to the left a wood, the wind whispering among the tender new leaves.

When she turned around the house was still there, shimmering as though it lay underwater.

"Stay there," she said to it and set off towards the wood, letting the odd sensation inside her draw her forward. There was a smell from somewhere that she recognized as woodsmoke.

She listened to the soft sounds of the wood: birdsong, leaves growing, the tiny noise of mice breathing in their sleep, the clatter and whirr of a startled wood-pigeon. *This way*, said a voice in her head, tugging her onwards.

Kate phoned David as soon as she got home.

"Maths again?" he said, answering.

"No, listen. I've just been talking to Erda. I asked her if she was sometimes in different times and she wasn't sure she understood, but she thought she might be." There was silence on the other end of the line for a few seconds. "David?"

"I was just thinking it through. It doesn't sound very definite, does it?"

"No, but ..."

"Do *you* think she understood you?"

"Yes. Maybe not exactly, but yes. David, I think that maybe she did have some sort of accident and she's come unstuck in time, or got stuck in the wrong time."

"David!"

"Yeah dad?"

"Christine's been calling you for tea."

"Sorry, I didn't hear."

"Come on."

"Okay. Kate: got to go. Talk to you later."

The phone went silent and Kate threw it down on her bed in frustration.

"Kate?"

"Yes, Mum?"

Her mother pushed the door open and stood there, obviously fuming.

"Where have you been?" Kate opened her mouth to reply but her mother cut her off. "You forgot, didn't you?"

Kate's hand flew to her open mouth as she remembered to her horror that she had been meant to come straight home from school to look after Ben so that her mum could get her hair cut.

"Oh no Mum, I'm sorry, I'm really sorry."

"Well, that doesn't really help does it? I've had to cancel the appointment and believe it or not, Ben was looking forward to going out somewhere with you."

"I'm sorry," Kate said again miserably.

"It's about time you started taking a bit more responsibility around here. You're not a child any more." Ruth turned on her heel and went out, closing the door hard behind her.

Kate threw herself on the bed and pulled the pillow down over her head.

The wood was beautiful, full of so many different things. Not like the city, where you could only hear people, drowning out everything else. Here she listened to the words of the trees and the birds, the mice and the fungi and the deer, words about sunlight and water and seeds and nests. It seemed to open in front of her, drawing her on. She was intrigued by the constant tug she felt and followed it, eager to find its source.

Morgan and Thomas had avoided entering the city and instead followed a route that took them round the south side of its walls following the line of the red sandstone crags and the little river that fed the loch. The few people they met glanced at them curiously, for their clothes were not the same as those of the inhabitants, but nor were they so different that they caused comment.

Morgan walked like a man in a dream, and though he said nothing Thomas felt a tight knot of anxiety for him in his stomach. He still couldn't imagine what

Morgan meant to do when he was finally able to confront the Stardreamer.

Just as he was thinking this, Morgan stopped, frowning, and stood still for several seconds, as though listening.

"He's not where he was. He's moving. This way." He set off between a straggle of buildings, heading south west now instead of due west. They soon left the buildings and the little fields behind and were back in uncultivated land, with springy heather underfoot and gorse and hazel around them.

Less than ten minutes later Morgan stopped again and gripped Thomas's arm. "He's closer. Can you feel him yet? He's coming to find us."

Thomas felt all his hair stand up. *I was wrong to come* he wanted to say. *Let's go back. Tell them we couldn't find him. Let's run away while we can.* He bit the words back and tried to look as though he felt calm. Morgan was depending on him to help ... somehow.

They walked on, towards destiny and doom.

Erda lay on her back in a clearing, watching drops of sunlight slide through the mosaic of leaves above her. She joined them for a little, moving with the breeze, feeling the warm sun feed her. She turned over and pushed her face into the grass, inhaling the green sappy scent, with the underlying smells of earthworm and beetle.

Refreshed, she got to her feet and went on. She was close to the source of the frail tugging now. Soon she would find where it came from.

Ahead of Morgan and Thomas was the edge of a great wood of birch and pine and oak. Many small paths led into it, but there was no obvious way to decide which, if any, was the main one. There was no sign here of any of the villagers, though the smell of charcoal-burning came out from the eaves of the forest.

Thomas put a hand on Morgan's arm. "Let's stop here for a while, rest and eat before we go in there. We want to be ready when we meet him."

Morgan nodded. "All right. That makes sense."

They sat with their backs against a nearby boulder and got out the cheese and dried apples and bread they carried. Thomas went off a little way to refill their water bottles from a stream. Morgan ate absently, his eyes on the wood.

Erda walked between the warm trunks of the trees, occasionally putting her hand on red-brown or silvery bark, feeling the slow movement of the tree's life beneath it.

Now that she was close, she could feel the consciousness behind the force that pulled her. It was a man, and he was aware of her as no one else in this world was. How could this be? No one else, not even Kate and David, with whom she had shared so many words, could see her like this. She walked a little faster.

Thomas packed away the last of the food and fastened his pack, talking of nothing to break the silence that seemed to grip Morgan. There was no alternative now but to go into the wood and face whatever lay in wait for them there.

He straightened up and shouldered the pack, looking back towards the town for anything that might reasonably distract Morgan from the wood.

"Look."

The single word froze Thomas momentarily. He raised his eyes slowly to Morgan's face, saw all the

colour gone from it and turned to look at whatever had
come for them.

At the edge of the wood stood a girl, just a girl,
slightly built, with long, dark-red hair and outlandish
clothes. As he looked, a sudden gust of wind ran out of
the wood around her, flattening the heather between
them.

Thomas found his voice.

"Is the Stardreamer with her?"

"She is the Stardreamer."

7. Falling

For some seconds, Thomas had no idea what to think or say, then he decided that it was impossible he had understood Morgan properly.

"What do you mean?"

Morgan didn't look round, his gaze locked into that of the girl who stood at the edge of the wood. "She is the Stardreamer."

"But she's just a girl. How can she be?"

"Can you not feel the power in her?"

Thomas shook his head. "No. It is you who can feel the Stardreamer's power, not me. Are you sure about this?"

Morgan nodded.

At the edge of the wood the girl raised her hand and pushed the hair back from her face and as she did so, Thomas thought he saw a brief flash of light behind or perhaps around her. She stepped out of the trees and walked towards them.

"What do we do now?"

His eyes still on the Stardreamer, Morgan smiled grimly. "We go to meet her, of course." He turned and looked at Thomas then and gave a sudden heart-felt grin. "Or we could turn and run, if you think you're fast enough."

"Faster than you anyway." Thomas rose to the bait automatically and the tension of the moment broke.

They walked to meet the unlikely figure of the Stardreamer.

As they drew closer together, Thomas began to feel, or to imagine, a tingling in his fingertips which spread all over his skin, a prickling. He shook himself like a dog.

"Now you feel it," said Morgan beside him.

To Erda, walking slowly out from the wood, it was as though she followed a shining thread now towards the man who knew her. He was tall, with brown hair and green eyes and clothes that were different from hers. A word she didn't recognize spun its way from his mind to hers.

Stardreamer.

She searched among the words she knew, but could find nothing to make sense of it.

The other man with him was a little shorter and more slightly built, with black hair and a fine-boned face. He seemed to be about the same age as she was, here, while the man who knew her was a few years older. She walked towards them through the sudden wind that had sprung up to run across the heather from the wood, watching the thread that linked her to the brown-haired man grow shorter and thicker. Five paces apart, they stopped and stood in silence, absorbing each other, each waiting for what the other would do.

In the end it was Erda who spoke first. "I felt you. You were looking for me."

Morgan swallowed and opened his mouth, but no words would come out.

"We thought you might need help. We thought you might be lost." Thomas didn't know what moved him to say it.

"Like Kate and David," said Erda. They looked at her uncomprehendingly. "They want to help me. They think I am in the wrong place."

"Are you?" asked Morgan quietly.

Erda thought. "Maybe. I don't know where I should be. Maybe here, maybe there." She shrugged. "You knew I was here." Morgan nodded. "Not you." She looked over at Thomas, who shook his head, then turned back to Morgan. "How did you know?"

"I'm not sure. I can feel if you are close or not, like ..." He cast about for something that would serve for comparison, "like a magnet."

"Magnet." She repeated the word, frowning at him slightly as she tried to make sense of what the word was telling her. It was very confusing. She would ask Kate and David. She turned her attention back to the men in front of her. "You found me. Now what will you do?"

Here we go, thought Thomas. *Now it all comes apart.* He braced himself for whatever was about to happen.

"We could go for a walk," said Morgan. "We could show you where we came from."

The all-powerful Stardreamer, the fragile girl in front of them, nodded her head smiling, and Thomas wondered anew if she was really what Morgan thought, or what she appeared to be.

That night, Tiger died. David had known with his head that it would happen one day soon. He was an old cat — fifteen and a bit — and for the last year or so he'd been losing weight. He'd always been a big lump of a cat, who dominated the others in the neighbourhood not because he was aggressive, but by sheer bulk, but recently he'd got scrawny; David could feel his hip bones and shoulder blades when he picked him up.

They'd taken him to the vet, who'd said he had kidney failure and given him some tablets that perked him up for a while, but lately he'd gone off his food and David had realized he wasn't going to live much longer, although he was still pottering about happily enough.

Even that afternoon he'd been out in the garden, lying slit-eyed in an unseasonably warm pool of sunlight, purring to himself while David lay on his stomach on the grass beside him, reading.

He'd jumped — a bit stiffly — up onto David's bed in the evening, as he always did, waiting to curl up next to him at bedtime, but sometime during the night he must have got down again and made his way to the spare bedroom.

David found him there the next morning, curled neatly up as though he was asleep; but it was instantly obvious he was dead.

"Dad! Come here — quick. It's Tiger."

They'd lifted him out from under the bed and laid him on his favourite cushion and stroked his fur smooth then looked, for the last time, at the wonderful shapes of the little pads on his paws and the elegant tufts of fur on his ears. Alastair had dug a grave under the apple tree and lined it with grass cuttings and they laid him in and covered him with a pillowcase so they wouldn't have to see the earth flatten his fur when they piled it back in and firmed the turf down again.

"He was a good old cat," said Alastair, "I remember Mum bringing him home. He was such a scrawny little kitten; we could never believe how big he got."

This was the beginning of a whole series of Tiger stories that they told each other regularly, like family fairy tales: "When Tiger got stuck in the chimney" and "When Tiger disappeared".

They stood on the dewy grass and told the stories again and laughed. Christine watched from an upstairs window and when she thought the time was right, came down to join them.

"Poor old Tiger," she said. "You know, we had lots of cats when I was small, but I think Tiger was the friendliest cat I ever met. He was really special."

David gave a watery smile. "You're right. He *was*

really special," he said, then went to his room to get ready for school so she wouldn't see him crying.

It wasn't just Tiger he'd lost, you see. It was another link to Mum gone. Tiger had been her cat; she'd chosen him and David felt that a memory of her lived on in the cat. Now that was gone too. He sat on his bed, wiping away tears with the heels of his hands. No one else would understand how he felt, not even Kate. He blew his nose and started downstairs.

Halfway down he stopped to listen to Dad and Christine talking.

"We'll get another cat of course," said Alastair.

"I like a cat around the place. I've always been used to them."

"I'll suggest it to David when he comes downstairs. We'll go and look for one at the Cat and Dog Home at the weekend."

"I don't think I'd say anything to David about a new cat just yet — give it a few days," said Christine.

"Why? You saw how upset he was about Tiger."

"That's the point. Tiger was his mum's cat, not just any cat. I don't think he'll feel that another cat can take his place just yet."

There was silence for a few seconds.

"Stupid. I should have thought of that myself. You're right of course. We'll leave it for a week or so."

David finished his journey downstairs more noisily than usual.

"Bye Dad, bye Christine. See you later."

He closed the front door behind him and set off for school. *Funny, how people could surprise you sometimes.*

Morgan's mind was in turmoil. He'd started this search expecting a hopeless confrontation with someone whose physical presence would embody the

Stardreamer's power. He'd assumed he would be some gigantic, terrifying figure. Instead Morgan was faced with this young and fragile girl, with the dark red hair and beautiful trusting face and eyes the colour of copper coins.

He had no idea what to do.

They walked together in a loose group, Thomas talking to the girl. Her answers were strange, sometimes like those of a child. Morgan himself felt as though he'd been struck dumb. It was clear she had no idea of her power, but Morgan could feel it in the air around them, crackling like fire.

"What is your name?"

The question roused him to speech at last.

"Morgan."

"And I am Thomas, his brother."

She looked from one to the other, her head tilted.

"Yes," she said. "I understand. I am Erda."

Erda. It was a strange name, one Morgan had never heard before, though why he found that surprising he couldn't say. Thomas had picked up a bit of wood somewhere and begun whittling it as they walked along. The girl watched his hands closely as he worked.

"What are you doing?"

"Making a bird."

"Out of wood? How can you change one to the other?"

Thomas laughed.

"Not a real one. A model." She looked at him, uncomprehending. "Like a picture."

"Ah, a picture." She nodded. That word meant something, though she still didn't fully understand. He meant something different from what she knew.

His hands moved so quickly that she couldn't follow them as he turned the wood to and fro, shaping it with the knife.

Morgan, meanwhile, was trying to imagine his way ahead. They would walk to the door in the cave by the chapel and step through into the Wildwood, then they would lead her to the Heart of the Earth and persuade her to step in. Somehow.

For the first time he felt disquiet about what he was planning to do. If he did it, this frail and powerful girl would be trapped forever in the Heart of the Earth, dreaming the Worlds safe. He had not expected to feel guilt at the prospect of succeeding.

"What is wrong?" Erda had stopped and turned her innocent golden gaze on him. "The thing that binds us ... it twists. Something troubles you."

He felt his heart give one great beat, like a hammer stroke.

"Nothing." He forced a smile. "There is nothing wrong. Look — the bird is nearly finished."

Thomas, who had stopped dead when Erda spoke, pulled himself together and turned his attention to the carving. A few seconds later, he handed Erda a little hawk, so swiftly carved as to be more of a sketch than a portrait, but somehow capturing the essence of the bird.

"It's for you."

"For me? I can keep it?" She was looking at it closely. When he nodded she tucked it away in a pocket.

Instead of leading them back exactly the same way he and Thomas had come, Morgan had chosen a route that skirted the southern edge of the town. He could see the chapel now and beyond it the dark slit of the cave mouth. His agitation grew as they drew closer.

"Let's stop here for a minute for a drink and a rest," he said.

Thomas looked at him in surprise, but Erda sat down immediately among the heather.

"Yes," she said, looking at Morgan. "Rest and you will feel better. In the film it says that."

"Film? What's that?"

"I watch it at the house. Kate and David showed me. Words, pictures ..." Her words died away, leaving Morgan and Thomas even more puzzled than they had been. She leaned over and pulled at the bow slung across Morgan's back. Thomas noticed how he flinched away when she touched him.

"What is this?"

"A bow."

"What is it for?"

"Shooting."

She shook her head. "I don't understand."

"I'll show you." He stood and unslung the bow, fitted an arrow and fired it, at nothing in particular, in the direction of the chapel.

"Let me try."

"All right, but ..."

She took the bow from his hand, and the arrow he offered, drew the bow and shot. The arrow landed a little further away than Morgan's had, Thomas noted.

"Why do you do this?"

"To hunt. Rabbits, deer ..."

"To stop life?" She seemed puzzled.

"Yes, for food. Some people do it for sport — to enjoy themselves."

"They enjoy stopping life? Strange. Does it not hurt them?"

It was Morgan's turn to look puzzled now. "No, how could it?"

But Erda didn't answer.

They walked on again, stopping to pick up the arrows as they went. It was early afternoon but as they drew near the chapel, there was no one in sight. They

paused for a moment and Erda looked down at the
town stretched along its rocky backbone below them.

"They do not have so many words now as in the
other time."

"Can you hear them?" asked Thomas, intrigued.

"The words come into my head." She tried to
explain.

"I hear them inside and the world tries to tell me
what they mean."

That, more than anything that had happened so far,
convinced Thomas that the girl was what Morgan
thought she was.

They were close to the cave mouth now, standing a
little way below the chapel.

"I will go back now," Erda announced.

"What?" said Morgan, hoping he had misunderstood.

"I like this place, but I will go back now."

"But you can't," said Thomas desperately.

"Why?"

"We want to show you our home," said Morgan
quickly. "It's just a little further. Please come." He put
a hand on her arm to draw her towards the cave
mouth, but she shook it off.

"No. I do not want to go with you."

"But you have to. Please." He grasped her arms and
started to pull her along with him.

"No!"

The shout seemed to rip the air. Impossible that it
should have come from the girl in his grasp. He rocked
on his heels as if a great gust of wind had shaken him
and began to pull her along again. Dimly he could hear
Thomas shouting at him to stop, but he couldn't. This
was what he had to do. It was part of who — of what —
he was.

The world shattered around him.

8. *Through the Door*

David told Kate about Tiger as they sat together in Geography that morning, colouring pictures of river systems. Kate had always been very fond of Tiger and was clearly upset by the news. David was relieved that she didn't immediately ask if he was going to get a kitten. He was about to tell her about Christine's unexpected insight into his feelings when all the lights flickered and there was a long rumble of thunder.

There was an excited mutter of conversation. Good storms were rare in Edinburgh; was this going to be one?

A moment later there was a flash of lightning so sudden and vivid that they all jumped and the loudest crack of thunder they had ever heard and all the lights went out.

Morgan spat out earth and bits of heather and opened his eyes. For a moment he had no idea where he was or what had happened and then, with a sickening lurch, memory returned. He sat up, wincing at the pain in his back and in his head and looked around. There was no sign of Thomas or the girl.

The chapel was a ruin.

At first he thought that Erda's blast of power had struck it, but as he looked he realized he was looking at something that had been ruined for a long time.

He struggled to his feet. Stretching away around him was a huge city, nothing like the town that had been there before.

So, she had blasted him through time and she and Thomas must be back where he had been minutes — or perhaps hours — before.

He had to get back, help Thomas. He would have to go back through to the briar glade and wait for the pool to change. Of course, they might already be there. Thomas might have succeeded where he had failed and be waiting for him anyway.

He could see the pack that Thomas had been carrying lying in the grass a little way off and went to pick it up before he went through the cave.

As he straightened with the pack, Morgan saw him, lying on his back near the bottom of the steep slope. He scrambled down like a man caught in a nightmare, willing him to sit up, to move, anything.

"Thomas?"

Thomas lay on his back, the empty sky reflected in his open eyes. Although Morgan knew already somewhere within himself that Thomas was dead he rubbed his hands and stroked his hair and called to him, then gathered him in his arms and listened to the sound of his own sobs.

She watched in silence, become the smallest thing she could, a ladybird on the tip of a grass blade, trying to understand. What had happened? Thomas's life had stopped. Had she done this? How? All she had done was push them away. She had not seen anyone whose life had stopped before.

His brother sobbed and rocked him in his arms as though it could undo what had happened. She knew it could not. Nothing could. When a life stopped it could not start again.

Morgan had no sense of the passing of time as he sat talking to Thomas, saying the things he'd never properly said when he was alive.

At last the words ran out. He laid Thomas down and closed his eyes, then gathered him up in his arms and got with difficulty to his feet. Willpower took him up the slope to the mouth of the cave. He did not look back as he stepped through, or notice the ladybird on his shoulder.

Abruptly, he was back in the briar glade. He traced the path outward between the thorny trunks and emerged into the Wildwood.

Tisian stood in the clearing, waiting for him, her face aged by grief. He heard her intake of breath as he stumbled to his knees and laid Thomas on the earth of his own world.

"You knew," said Morgan.

"I felt him die," replied Tisian, "as though someone had ripped a hook through my heart."

"That's not what I mean," continued Morgan wearily. "You knew before we went, didn't you?"

"I see possibilities, nothing more."

"You tried to warn us. But why didn't you make it clearer?"

"It was not clear to me. In any case, Thomas would still have gone if his fate demanded it."

"*Fate?*" He gave a bitter laugh.

"Don't laugh at fate. If you don't believe in it, why are you doing this? I know the answer; don't lie to me. You feel you are bound to this because you are your father's son. Perhaps Thomas too believed he was bound in some way. His death may have a purpose that we don't yet see."

"Purpose?" Morgan's grief exploded into anger. "What purpose could it possibly serve? I led him to his doom and that is something I must live with."

The ladybird flew from his shoulder to a crack in the bark of a nearby tree.

They buried Thomas near a rowan tree, digging the grave together, their argument put aside for the

moment, and burned a twist of herbs and a pine
branch on it as was the custom.

"Will you not stay here with me for a while?" asked
Tisian.

Morgan shook his head. "No. I must go back and
find her. This is not yet finished."

"Rest first. At least wait until morning." Her hair
had come down as they dug and hung halfway to her
waist.

"No." He got to his feet and they faced each other
over the grave. "I must go now. She may not be too far
away."

She could see that there was no point in trying to
dissuade him. Instead she walked with him to the edge
of the briar glade. "Take care," she said.

"Why?" he asked as he disappeared along the path.

The glade would not let him reach the pool. The
path wound around and about, but would not bring
him to it. He forced his way between the rose vines
until his arms were torn, trying to cut a way through
with his hunting knife. At last, he reached the pool,
only to find it was overgrown with an impenetrable
tangle of wrist thick stems. It was impossible to reach
it. He let out a howl of frustration and forced his way
out, no longer feeling the thorns tear his flesh.

When he emerged again, Tisian was still there. She
said nothing.

"The Door has closed to me," he panted. "I have to
go back. I must go to the Empty Place. They will send
me there."

"No! Not that way."

"There is nothing else I can do. The other Doors are
too far away. I must go back before I lose her trail."

She held up a hand. He could see her struggling with
herself.

"Wait. There is another way. There is a Door you know nothing of. In my house."

"Your house? But ..."

"Why do you think I choose to live out in the Wildwood away from everything? I was set to guard it long ago, but now comes the time it was made for. I cannot pretend any more that it is not." She sighed. "I am late in life to come to fear, but it seems I must. I had hoped that this would not happen in my time of Guardianship." She said no more and he was too weary and sick at heart to question her further just then.

They walked back to the house in silence, Tisian twisting her hair back up into its untidy knot. Walking behind her, Morgan saw the earth stains on her green and blue skirt from Thomas's grave and had to stop, his hand on a tree, while he caught his breath again.

The sagging door of Tisian's house stood open, as it always did. He followed her in, both of them ducking under the lintel.

After the bright afternoon light outside it took Morgan's eyes a moment to adjust to the relative gloom. He had been here many times before, but now he looked about him as though seeing it all for the first time; the bed with its patchwork quilts set in an alcove, the shelves of cooking pots and dried herbs and things that had caught Tisian's fancy when she was out walking in the wood: pine cones and feathers and birds' eggs and seed heads and a score of other things. More patchworks hung on the walls, so that from the inside it seemed as much a tent as a house.

"Wait for morning," she entreated him again.

"No. I must go now. Show me how."

She lifted aside one of the patchwork hangings and there was a door of blonde wood with an iron latch. He turned to her before he lifted the latch.

"Thank you. I will come back, don't worry." A small spider clung to his boot as he opened the door and stepped through.

Tisian closed it behind him and let the patchwork fall, then went to the window and stood, looking out at nothing, for a long time.

The lights had gone out all over Edinburgh and the power had stayed off for the best part of two hours. The lightning must have struck some crucial part of the supply network, the staff said.

Kate found herself strangely unsettled by it. She didn't mind thunder and lightning at all — liked them in fact — but just thinking about *this* thunder and lightning made a shudder run down her spine. For some reason it made her worry about her family, her friends. She couldn't throw off a feeling of foreboding, even when the lights went back on at last.

It wasn't until they met up again at lunchtime (emergency sandwiches because of the power cut) that she found it had had the same effect on David.

"Cats are meant to know when there's going to be a storm," said Kate. "Maybe this is the same sort of thing, but in reverse, sort of. There are ions or something in the air and we're sensitive to them."

"Mmmn ..." David didn't sound convinced.

The feeling had passed by the end of school and they dropped round to Mr Flowerdew's on their way home as planned, to water the plants and drop off some food for Erda.

There was no sign of her, which was not unusual, but it brought the sense of foreboding back into Kate's mind.

"I'm sure she's okay, but we can come back tomorrow before football and check," said David.

"What time's your match?"

"Ten. What about you?"

"The same, but it's just a practice."

They locked the door behind them and headed home.

He stepped into a small room in another house, brighter than Tisian's. There was a large window with thin white curtains, a chair, a big wooden cupboard and a bed. He went to the window and moved the curtain aside to look out. There were houses all around him, some three or four storeys high and a street below the window with the strange smelly vehicles he recognized as cars from his few previous visits to this place and time.

He let the curtain fall back and sat down on the bed, his head in his hands, overwhelmed again. He was so tired. He lay down for a moment before he went out in search of Erda and exhausted and sick at heart, was asleep in seconds.

The spider let itself down from the bed on a silken thread and a few seconds later Erda stood there, watching Morgan in silence. She took the little hawk that Thomas had made and laid it beside him on the bed.

What have I done? She asked in the silence of her mind. *What am I?*

You are the Stardreamer, the house said.

9. First Aid

"What have you got?" asked Kate when she met David the next morning.

"Milk, rolls, eggs and a sweatshirt of Christine's out of the washing pile."

"Mmmn ... nice. I've got cereal and pasta and mushroom sauce and more underwear."

They walked down the hill. It was already hot although it was only quarter past nine. "Glorious summer in prospect", said some of the comments in the papers, while others talked glumly of "irreversible climate change due to global warming", all because for once, Kate's dad said, they were having a decent spring.

They let themselves in and picked up a couple of letters that had arrived for Gordon. In the hall, the big grandfather clock that had stopped on Mr Flowerdew's death looked down on them soundlessly.

Usually Erda came right away from wherever she was to see them when she heard them arrive, but today there was no sign of her and no sound. Kate called her name and a few seconds later heard noises from one of the bedrooms.

Morgan opened his eyes and was baffled at first by his surroundings. He lay still, waiting to remember and when he did, wished he could forget again. He sat up slowly, with some difficulty. His whole body felt stiff and battered, buffeted by the blast of power that had killed Thomas. He could hear voices coming from somewhere else in the house. How long had he been asleep? His hand brushed against something and he looked down. Thomas's hawk lay on the cover of the bed beside him. It took him a moment to put things together and realize that Erda must have been here.

The voices came again from somewhere below. He went to the door and opened it, wondering if he would find himself looking at the back of Tisian's patchwork, but in front of him he found a bright hallway with several doors opening off it, the top of a stairway visible at the far end, voices floating up to him.

Morgan went along the hall and started down the stairs, which curved around to the left. As he came round the curve he found himself confronted by a boy and a girl, not children, but not grown yet either. The girl had fair hair, cut short to her shoulders, and the boy was dark. They were staring at him with wide eyes and open mouths. Suddenly he realized what he must look like, torn and bloody and wild, appearing without warning in their world.

"Don't be frightened," he said. "I don't mean you any harm."

Kate and David looked up as they heard footsteps coming along the hall and down the stairs, but instead of Erda they found themselves looking at a man, a complete stranger. He had longish dark hair and wore clothes of green and brown: trousers tucked into boots, a shirt with a jacket-jerkin thing over it. They were all tattered and stained with earth and what looked like blood. The man's face and hands were scratched and smeared with blood too. He looked awful.

"Who are you?" asked David.

"What happened to you?" asked Kate.

They had all spoken at once.

"We're not frightened," said Kate, almost sure she wasn't, in spite of the man's appearance. "If the house let you in, you're probably okay."

"We were just expecting someone else to come down the stairs," said David. "You surprised us." That was true anyway.

"I came through a Door from ... another place and was here," said the man. "Up there." He pointed back up the stairs.

"What happened to you?" repeated Kate. "How did you get hurt?"

Morgan sat down heavily on a step, lost for words. The boy and girl came closer, concern in their eyes.

"Are you all right?" asked David.

He passed a hand over his eyes. "No."

"Can we help?" asked Kate.

He lifted his head and looked properly into their faces, for some reason fearing a trick, but he saw nothing but puzzlement and honest concern.

"Are you hungry? Thirsty?" she continued.

How long was it since he'd last eaten a meal? He couldn't remember. He nodded.

"We've got food. Come into the kitchen and sit down and we'll get you something."

He followed them obediently down the stairs. The girl stopped at a door.

"You might want to wash some of the blood off your face."

He nodded and went into the room she showed him and watched her run the water. There was a mirror on the wall and when she left him alone he stared at his reflection blankly. He hadn't realized how bad he looked, wild-eyed like a madman. It was a wonder they hadn't turned and run as soon as they saw him. He rubbed at the blood on his hands and face until most of it was gone, pulling out a couple of thorns that had stuck deep. A few of the scratches started to bleed again and he dabbed at them with a towel. After a while he gave up and followed a trail of sound through to the kitchen.

"Sit down. There's some tea for you. The food's nearly ready."

There was a mug on the table, steam rising from it. He sat and drank. It was hot and sweet and he wrapped his cold hands round it as he drank.

They'd made him toast and scrambled eggs and they sat opposite him as he ate ravenously and in silence.

"Thank you," he said when he had finished.

"Your face is still bleeding," said David. "Do you want some plasters?"

Morgan looked at him, baffled.

"We've done First Aid at school. We could do it for you," added Kate.

Morgan absorbed this incomprehensible statement in silence, which they took for agreement. Kate went for the First Aid box while David poured more tea. He let them clean the bleeding cuts on his face and arms and stick little pink bandages over them.

"Well, at least you look better now," said the boy.

"Thank you. I should explain why I am here."

I should explain. I should explain ... what? I hunt the most powerful being in the Worlds, one who has killed my brother. How do I explain that to them?

"My name is Morgan," he began.

"We should have told you our names," said the girl. "I'm Kate and this is David."

Kate and David?

Kate and David showed me ...

He was thrown into fresh confusion. What did this mean? Were they the same people Erda had spoken of and if so ... He couldn't order his thoughts.

They were looking at him expectantly. He had said he would explain. What should he tell them now?

"Are you from another time?" the girl — Kate — blurted out.

"What?" Morgan was taken aback. "No — no."

"You said you came through a door from another place," she persisted.

"Yes, I did. Not another time, another place — another world."

He saw them exchange a quick glance.

"What do you mean?" asked David.

"On this planet there are three worlds: yours, which you call Earth, mine, which my people call the Wildwood and the hidden world, the Underworld. There are Doors between these worlds. In this house is one between your world and mine."

"Can *anyone* go through it?"

"No. Only certain people have the ... gift. My brother and I ..."

"Is he here too?" interrupted David.

"No. He died."

They muttered awkward words of sympathy which trailed back into silence.

"Why did you need to get to our world?" said David quietly.

"I'm looking for someone," he said carefully, and saw them exchange that glance again. With every moment that passed he grew more convinced that these were the same Kate and David that Erda had spoken of. "You are not like the others I have met when I have been in this world before," he said, playing for time. "You come and go in this house, you hardly seem surprised by what I tell you ... What are you?"

"Nothing. Nothing special," replied Kate. "We're just people. Teenagers. But we've ... seen things. And the man who owned it left us keys to the house when he died so that we could come and go when we wanted to."

"The Guardian is dead?" Morgan was shocked. "When? How did it happen?"

David ignored his questions and replied with another. "You knew him? Mr Flowerdew?"

"I do not know that name. To me he was the Guardian. I met him twice when I came to this world through another Door, a few years ago. He brought me to this house once. Until today I did not know there was a Door that led here. I wonder if he did?"

"He died about a year and a half ago," said Kate. "In a battle against the Lords of Chaos."

The boy had become very still, Morgan noticed, as though it caused him pain to remember.

"You say you are ordinary, but you talk about the Lords and the Guardians as familiar beings. How many in your world do this?"

"Not many, I suppose." Kate gave a rueful smile.

"Has no new Guardian come?"

David shrugged. "Not as far as we know. Would we know?"

"He would be here if there was one."

"Maybe they've decided Edinburgh's safe after what happened before, so they don't think we need one."

His slow brain had finally caught up with the conversation and he realized this must be the Kate and David that Erda had spoken of, and that they couldn't have seen her since his disastrous encounter with her, or they would already know all about him.

"I said I was looking for someone. It is a young woman who is in your world, but does not belong here."

Kate's eyes widened. "Do you know her name?"

"Yes. She is called Erda."

He heard Kate draw a sharp breath.

"We were right then."

"What do you mean?" asked Morgan, feigning ignorance. "Do you know her?"

"Yes," said David. "We met her in this house. We thought she didn't belong here. We thought maybe she'd had an accident and lost her memory or something. Does she come from your world then?"

"Not from my world, no, but I want to take her to where she belongs. It is true she scarcely knows who she is."

"Thank goodness there's someone who can take her home. Her family must be so worried," said Kate, frowning.

Morgan was taken aback to find that they thought of Erda in this way.

"I do not think she has any family," he said, not really knowing why.

"Poor thing," Kate said. "Still, at least she's got us now, hasn't she?"

Erda soared high above the city, looking through a falcon's eyes at the pattern of streets and parks and buildings below. Somewhere down there were Kate and David and Morgan. Morgan, whose brother's life she had stopped, somehow.

The World had told her she was the Stardreamer, but what did that mean and what did Morgan want from her?'

10. The Letter

Two days passed and there was still no sign of Erda. David and Kate couldn't help but worry; she was almost like a child — how would she cope alone?

"It's like knowing Ben's out there on his own," said Kate, shaking her head at the thought.

Morgan too had gone, leaving later the same morning that they had met him to search for her.

School swallowed them up. Kate had tests in maths and chemistry and did badly in both. Her mother decided she needed "A Talk."

"You may not think what you do now matters ..."

"But I ..."

"But it does. You set habits now that will stay with you all the way through school, bad or good ones. You spend time shut up in your room and say you're working, but you've got that music on and you can't really be concentrating."

"I *am*. It helps me concentrate."

"Why aren't you getting better marks then?"

"Because I don't understand maths and there's lots of maths in chemistry. I'm okay at English and biology and geography and things, but you never ..."

"You've got to put effort into all your subjects you know, not just the ones you enjoy."

Kate gave up. It was clear her mother wasn't going to listen to anything she said.

"From now on you can do your schoolwork in the kitchen like Ben, before you disappear off to your bedroom."

"But I can't concentrate with him wittering on. You're *so* unfair! You're making it worse."

She stormed out of the sitting room and her bedroom door made the pictures jump on the walls as she slammed it shut.

"That went well, don't you think?" said her dad.

"Oh, shut up!" snapped Ruth.

Ever since she'd been so understanding about his feelings for Tiger, things had been going better between David and Christine, partly because he now gave her the benefit of the doubt instead of leaping to the worst possible conclusion about her intentions all the time.

One evening a few days after the encounter with Morgan, David and Christine sat in the garden. Alastair was trying to light the barbecue while Christine and David enjoyed a cool drink in the shade. It was ridiculously hot for May.

They'd been talking amicably about school and what subjects David thought he might choose to study, when Christine asked, out of the blue, "How long has Claire looked after you now?"

"Four and a half years," he said, though she must already know that. Why was she asking?

"She's great, isn't she? I know how fond you two are of each other." David made a sort of grunt which was meant to signal agreement without condoning the use of a word as wet as *fond*. "I was just wondering," she went on. "You're thirteen, you hardly need anyone to look after you any more, so there's not much for Claire to do ..."

David put his glass down so hard that it toppled over on the paving, a trail of sticky coke spreading from it.

"No! How could you?" He was looking at her in horror. "I thought you were okay, I thought you understood and all this time you've been planning to get rid of Claire." He pushed himself to his feet, scarlet with anger, afraid he would burst into tears.

"No, David, you're wrong — I didn't mean ..."

But he wasn't listening. He turned and half ran into the house.

Alerted by the noise, Alastair left the smoking barbecue and came over.

Christine gave a sigh, a rueful expression on her face. "Well, I messed that up completely."

"It's not your fault. He just leapt to conclusions. Maybe I should have told him; I just thought it might work better coming from you."

"I didn't even get that far and now he hates me again. Are we ever going to sort things out?"

"It'll come right." He gave her a kiss. "You'll see."

One by one, the Great Ones stepped through into the Underworld, donning their physical bodies as they did so.

The Queen of Darkness was clad in a gown the colour of old blood and a crown of jet and garnets. She had been hunting and carried a small, deeply curved black bow.

The Lightning King was in his usual robes of tattered black, a few forgotten tendrils of lightning slithering across it like tiny snakes.

Tethys the Water Witch wore a dress of shifting iridescent rainbow, like oil on water. A pool of water grew about her feet as she stood waiting with the others.

"Where are the wolves?" asked the King.

The two wolves which often accompanied Tethys were absent.

"With the Hunt," she replied.

A few minutes passed before the Hunter appeared among them. Unconsciously, they all drew back a little from him.

It was difficult to say what he wore: rags and tatters of cloth and skin that clothed him without being garments. His bare torso and arms were flecked with blood, as were his owl-eyed face and the horns, much like those of a roe deer, that grew among his chestnut hair.

"Is the hunt over?" asked the Queen.

"Yes." He smiled a terrible smile. "A good hunt. The wolves will feed well." He slid a black knife back into its sheath at his side.

"We must decide what to do now," said the Queen. "We were close for a moment when she killed the man Thomas. I thought the power might overwhelm her then. But it did not. Now she knows she possesses it and begins to understand what it can do. She will be on her guard and our task will be harder. Everything is at stake. Now that the Stardreamer has been called, there can be no going back."

"She must be brought to the Heart of the Earth if we are to use her power to destroy it," said the King.

"My son will bring her," said the Hunter.

"Or if he fails," mused the Queen, "perhaps we can use the children. It may prove to be very useful that she fell into their hands. Making them the instruments for the destruction of their world would be a fitting way to repay them for thwarting our plans before."

"We must break into their world if we are to reach the Wildwood and the Heart of the Earth," said a voice thin and chilly as a blade. When the Hunter spoke, everyone listened.

"We must be invited for that to happen," said the Queen cautiously. "Those two know us for what we are. We cannot disguise ourselves from them."

"We can influence others around them though: draw them to one of the places where the barriers have grown thin, trick them into saying the words ... We grow stronger every day the Stardreamer is here," mused the King.

"Most people are much easier to influence than those children," said Tethys, smiling a scarlet smile. "We must watch for a little, decide who and where, then persuade them to the right place ..."

They pretended to go to Badminton Club but went to the house instead. It was now four days since Erda had disappeared and Morgan had gone after her and there had been no sign of either. They didn't hold out much hope that anyone would be there now and the house felt very empty when they opened the front door.

There was a postcard from Gordon though. *Great weather and good golf courses but I'm playing rubbish! Getting brown (that's a first!) Hope the plants are behaving!* He hadn't put any names on, just the house number, but they knew it was for them.

They decided to go to Badminton Club after all; they would only be ten minutes late and if they went there would be no chance of their parents discovering what they were doing.

As they turned back to the front door, David noticed something odd.

"Look, the door's open." It was the door of the big, silent grandfather clock he was referring to. It stood slightly ajar. "Was it like that when we came in?"

"I don't think so," said Kate. "I'm sure we'd have noticed. It's always shut." She tried to push it closed but it wouldn't stay and something prevented it from closing far enough to turn the key. "There's something jamming it," she said.

"Let's see," said David, reaching inside. "There's a bit of paper stuck in the hinge. Wait a minute." He peered inside and wiggled at something. "There we go." He pulled it out.

Kate shut the door and turned the key.

"Kate," said David from behind her in a strange voice. "Look."

She turned. He was holding a small, cream-coloured envelope. On it was written clearly in Mr Flowerdew's writing: *For Kate and David*.

They stared at the envelope, then at each other.

"Well, open it," said Kate after a moment.

David tore open the envelope and unfolded the single sheet of paper it contained and they pored over it together.

My dear Kate and David,

I hope you will never have to read this letter, but if you have found it, it is because you must know what it will tell you, to be able to deal with what is happening.

If you are reading this, it means the Stardreamer has been called down by the Guardians or the Lords. I have always counselled against such a thing: the risk is too great, but if this letter has come to you it must have happened.

The Guardians hope to lock the Stardreamer's power into the place we call the Heart of the Earth. If we succeed the Lords will finally be defeated and the Worlds will be held safe in the Stardreamer's dreaming.

The Lords hope to provoke the Stardreamer into detonating all that power outside the Heart of the Earth and destroying it. Then the Guardians will be defeated utterly, and both time and the Worlds that make up this planet will be torn apart.

People will be searching for the Stardreamer and it is likely that one or more of them will pass through this house. Trust your instincts if you meet with any of them.

Unless it is locked within the Heart of the Earth the Lords of Chaos can feed off the Stardreamer's power. They may even be able to take physical form in your world.

Now to the hardest part; you will find it hard to forgive me for not telling you before. You were able to help in the defeat of the Lords because you were descendants of the Smith. This you already know, but not quite why it was so. The Smith was what we call a Child of Light; one of his ancestors was a Guardian. His blood runs in your veins and so you are also Children of the Light.

That might please you, but not this; you are also Children of the Dark, for somewhere in your past one of the Lords of Chaos was your ancestor.

You are Children of Light and Darkness, poised between the two; that was why the Lords could appear in your dreams. Both sides will seek you out now and the Lords will be trying to find a way into your world.

The final conflict is upon us and you must choose what you will do and who you will help. The Lords will tell you that you would survive the destruction of time and the Worlds. That is true, because of the Darkness that is part of you.

I am truly sorry to weigh you down with this knowledge, but you cannot fight without it and soon you will need to.

Your friend,
John Flowerdew

The letter stunned them into silence for a long time. They read it over and over, sure at first that they must have misunderstood, but gradually finding themselves unable to disbelieve.

Children of Light and Darkness.

The Lords of Chaos had tried to destroy their world once and they had fought against them and helped defeat them, but they hadn't known then that part of them was the same as the Lords.

"How could he not tell us?" Kate asked in a whisper. "How can we be like *them*?"

David's hand trembled as he held the letter.

"What do we do? There's no one to help us, Kate. We have to work it out for ourselves."

11. Into the Woods

Morgan hunted the Stardreamer across the Worlds. *She is here somewhere. I feel her presence,* he had said to Kate and David as he left them and it was as he had said it that he realized he had been aware of that presence when he took Thomas's body back to the Wildwood to bury him and came back through Tisian's Door. She had been with him all the time, unseen, and now her presence was like a background noise grown so familiar you didn't notice it until it stopped. She was moving between worlds, slipping away from him again and again, and each time she moved out of the world he was in it seemed to lurch as though he had lost his sense of balance.

She watched him, getting as close as she could without him realizing exactly where she was. She had listened to him talk to Tisian about her, trying to understand what was this thing — Stardreamer — that she was. The word made pictures in her head that she didn't yet comprehend: a great void between the stars, a glittering cave, a little meadow of parched grass high on a hillside.

She knew she was dangerous.

The cuts on Morgan's face and hands healed, though the hurt of Thomas's death was as raw as ever. He pursued Erda with no idea of what he would do if he was faced with her. Try to kill her? Reason with her? Confess?

He knew that Thomas's death had been an accident, but if he couldn't blame her for it, he would have to take all the blame on himself. He was afraid of doing that.

Every few days he would pass through Tisian's house and she would make him eat and sleep and talk to her. Otherwise, he seemed to have almost lost the use for speech. He saw no one he knew and avoided as much contact with people as was possible.

He felt as though he was the hunted, not the hunter.

They sat at the kitchen table in silence, Gordon's postcard and the explosive letter laid in front of them.

"Final conflict?" said Kate in disgust. "I thought everything we went through last time was meant to keep time safe."

"It was," said David. "Read it again. This is something he thought would never happen, something he'd argued with the other Guardians about. If he'd really thought this was going to happen don't you think he'd have told us himself about being Children of Light and Darkness, so he could have explained it properly and answered our questions? He never thought we'd need to read that letter. It was just …"

"Insurance?"

"Yes. Exactly."

"And why do we have to get involved? Wasn't last time enough? Why not Gordon — he lives in the house after all," Kate went on angrily.

"Yes, but he's not here just now, is he?" said David gently, "and it seems to be now that this is happening."

Kate put her head in her hands.

"I want a *normal* life, with *normal* worries, not this again — and we don't even have Mr Flowerdew this time." David said nothing. "Why aren't you angry? And why are you so quiet? Are you just going to accept it?"

David sighed. "What choice do we have, Kate? We're trapped in this; it doesn't matter if we think it's fair or not."

They sat, not speaking, for a few moments.

"Stardreamer ... Heart of the Earth ..." muttered David. "No clue what any of it means."

"Maybe he left other letters — clues — somewhere," said Kate excitedly, pushing her chair back and standing up.

They ran to the grandfather clock and unlocked it to look inside, feeling around the dark corners, checking underneath and behind it.

Nothing.

"What about the study?" Kate said.

They hurried up the two flights of stairs to Mr Flowerdew's study and opened the door.

It had lain largely undisturbed since his death, aside from a little light dusting on Gordon's part. The telescope and binoculars still stood waiting by the window, the notebooks and watercolours stacked ready on the shelves and the stuffed Tawny Owl keeping watch with cold yellow eyes.

Kate looked around at the organized clutter of belongings, wondering where to start.

"Desk drawers?" she suggested. David nodded and they began to carefully go through anything that might contain a clue about the information in the letter.

After almost an hour they had found nothing. Kate sat back on her heels, a smudge of dust on her nose and pushed her hair behind her ears, thinking.

"I'm an idiot," she announced.

"I know," said David, head in a cupboard, "but I haven't told anyone else."

"You are as well." He pulled his head out of the cupboard and looked at her. "Erda. And Morgan. You don't really believe it's a coincidence that they turn up just before this letter shows itself?"

David hit his forehead with the heel of his hand.

"How could I not think of that?"

"Beats me," said Kate absently, thinking again. "I know what I think. I think they're both looking for this Stardreamer person ... thing ... and Erda found it and got hurt and lost her memory. Now Morgan's looking for her to take her home and then he'll go looking for the Stardreamer too."

"Maybe ..." David considered this. "Why didn't he tell us though?"

"He'd only just met us, he doesn't know anything about us. He probably thinks we're just kids and we wouldn't understand."

They looked at each other. David shrugged.

"We have to help them."

"I know," said Kate with a sigh. "How can we help them though, if we don't even know where they are?"

"Erda will come back here, surely?"

"Probably. Maybe. Oh, I don't know. But what about Morgan? He talked about a Door in this house that led to somewhere else. Maybe we can find him."

"We'll have to find the Door first. Does he really mean a door? Maybe it'll look like something else. Or maybe it won't open for us."

"Well, there's no harm in looking anyway. He came down from upstairs when we met him, but he was in one of the rooms on the first floor, not up here. Come on."

They went in and out of the bedrooms and bathrooms, opening and closing the doors to the rooms and to the big cupboards and the wardrobes.

Nothing.

They sat side by side on the single bed in the smallest bedroom.

"Well, we tried. It looks as though we'll have to wait for one of them to come back," David sighed. He looked at his watch. It was nearly eleven. "I suppose I'd better go home and see what Christine's decided to do now. Maybe she's sold the house since I went out."

They got up and opened the door. In front of them hung a piece of cloth with blocks of patchwork colour. They took a step back, staring at each other, wide-eyed, silent.

Kate swallowed. "It looks as though we've found it."

They crept forward and stood perfectly still behind the cloth, listening intently, but there was no sound. They knelt and peered under the edge where it finished a few inches above the floor.

The room they were looking into was dim compared with the bedroom. They could see a beaten earth floor and an open fire with a black pot hanging over it. There was a smell of soup.

"D'you think that's Morgan's house?" whispered Kate.

"Maybe."

They peeked round the edges of the patchwork and, seeing no one, stepped out into the other room. As their eyes adjusted to the change of light they saw colour everywhere: patchworks hung on the walls and spread over the bed in its alcove, the glowing fire with the soup bubbling over it, the stacked shelves with their carefully sorted flotsam. It reminded Kate immediately of Mr Flowerdew's study.

The outside door scraped on a bump in the earth floor as someone pulled it open, making Kate and David jump. They drew closer together, unsure what to do or say. A tall woman was coming in, ducking under the lintel. She wore a dress patched with colour on colour, red and green and blue and brown. Her hair was grey-brown, twisted up on top of her head and seemingly held in place with a couple of twigs. There was a white clay pipe in her mouth.

She looked at them quietly for a few seconds then took the pipe from her mouth, moving slowly as though they were wild animals that might take fright and run at any moment.

"Hello," she said, moving towards the hearth. "Soup's ready if you'd like some."

They nodded dumbly. She pointed them towards a couple of chairs at the table and they sat silently as she ladled soup into bowls and set it down in front of them.

"Here," she said, handing each of them a spoon. "Eat it while it's hot."

David hesitated, remembering stories where it was important not to eat in Fairyland or you wouldn't be able to return home. *Don't be stupid,* he told himself, *wherever you are it's not Fairyland. Anyway, Kate's eating it.* He swallowed a few spoonfuls.

Whatever else the soup was going to do it seemed to have given them back the power of speech.

"You probably want to know what we're doing in your house," began Kate.

The woman shook her head. "Not really. I suppose you came through the Door — from the other place that is, not the front door."

"Yes. We were looking for some people — friends of ours."

"Oh yes," said Tisian, "and what would their names be?"

They were silent again. How much should they tell her? *Trust your instincts,* thought Kate. *That's what the letter said.* She looked pointedly at David, who gave a tiny nod.

"There's a girl called Erda and a man called Morgan."

She nodded. "Then you'll be David and Kate. My name is Tisian."

They gasped. "How do you know that?" breathed David.

"Morgan told me."

"Then you know him! Where is he? Has he found Erda?" he went on, the questions tumbling out.

"He is searching for the Stardreamer."

"Yes," Kate brushed the comment aside. "We know about the Stardreamer, but has he found Erda?"

Tisian looked at them blankly.

"You do not know," she whispered.

"What?" they both asked.

Tisian looked from Kate to David and back before she answered.

"Your friend Erda ... she *is* the Stardreamer."

"What?" said David, unable to believe his ears.

"That's impossible," said Kate. "The Stardreamer is some sort of awesome, powerful being. Erda is ... just Erda. She's just a girl."

"That's exactly what Morgan thought when he met her. Oh dear, there's a lot he hasn't told you, isn't there?"

So she told them slowly, taking her time, picking her words carefully so the children had a chance to take it in slowly, bit by bit. Finally she told them about Thomas and how he had died and watched in sympathy as they tried to deal with that; that Erda, who they thought they knew, had that much power and had killed, albeit by accident.

There was silence in the room for a long time after she stopped talking. After a while David stirred and looked up.

"I knew too."

"What?" asked Kate, puzzled.

"When the Stardreamer arrived. I remember it now. I was having this dream about Mum. We were in

Princes Street Gardens and she was listening, then she said, 'She's coming. You must go.' and I woke up. It was the night after Gordon went away on holiday."

Kate gasped. "And I dreamed about Tethys' wolves that night, over and over. It was horrible, I hadn't dreamed about them in ages."

David suddenly realized how long they'd sat in the patchworked room. "Kate, we'll have to go. Our parents will be going spare."

"Yes, all right. Tisian, what should we do?"

"I do not know, my dear. You must do what your heart tells you."

"Can we come back?"

"If the Door will open for you. It is unpredictable."

"Tell Morgan ... tell him you told us and ask him to come back through to our world. Perhaps we can help him."

Tisian nodded.

"Kate, come on!"

Tisian lifted the cloth aside to reveal the pale door. David lifted the iron latch and opened it as the hanging fell back in place behind them and ...

... they were back in the smallest bedroom of Mr Flowerdew's house.

They looked at the familiar white-painted door and opened it half expecting to find themselves in Tisian's house again, but instead there were the landing and stairs, where they should be.

"Come on, let's go," said David, glancing at his watch. He looked again. According to his watch it was exactly eleven. He held it to his ear, heard the familiar tick. "Wait. What time is it?"

"Dunno. I forgot my watch. We can look at the kitchen clock."

It said eleven as well. They looked at each other.

"How long were we there?" asked David, although he already knew.

"An hour? An hour and a half? Definitely not less than an hour."

"I don't understand."

"Me neither. At least we're not in trouble for being late now though ..."

12. In the Underworld

Morgan walked the Underworld. He had only been here a few times before and was always glad to leave. Parts of it reminded him of the Wildwood, but as though seen in a subtly distorting mirror. It was difficult to say what made it so unsettling a place: the rivers seemed like ordinary rivers (if there were such things), the trees like normal trees and yet ...

The closest he could come when he'd once tried to describe it to Thomas, was that things seemed to have settled into the form they held just before he looked at them, as though they changed to fit his expectations, and gave him the queasy impression that they drifted into being something quite different when his attention strayed from them. He supposed it wasn't surprising that, in a World where the Lords of Chaos could come and go at will, things should seem so loosely anchored in reality.

He moved cautiously through the not-quite-shifting landscape, waiting for a glimpse of Erda. He could tell she was close by. The thread of power that bound them seemed to grow stronger by the day. Now he knew that she often shifted from her human shape and would sometimes creep close in the guise of a bird or insect, although he couldn't yet pick her out in those forms.

But I will, he thought, *soon.*

He stopped for a while at what passed here for midday, eating and drinking sparingly from the supplies he had brought with him. He never ate or drank anything that came from the Underworld, lest he find himself trapped there.

He closed his eyes for a few minutes after he had

eaten. He was always tired now — he didn't know why — and fell asleep almost at once dreaming of Thomas, as he often did. But today Thomas wouldn't talk to him. Instead he walked away from Morgan with a brown-haired woman in boots and trousers and a red top.

He walked on through the afternoon in woodland patched with light and shade until he came to a thickly wooded ravine. After walking along the edge for a while he realized he would have to climb down and up again. He found a place where traces of a path cut down through the trees, and looked across the gorge before starting down.

She was there! She stood at the other edge of the ravine directly opposite him, less than a stone's throw away. On level ground he could have covered the distance in a dozen strides. He found his bow was in his hands half-drawn, an arrow strung, before he even realized he had moved.

She stood quite still. He drew the bow further, aiming at her heart, his breath coming painfully.

"You killed my brother!" he shouted at her.

I know, she said without speaking. The words were simply there in his head. *I did not know what I was. No one told me. I did not mean to hurt either of you.*

"I know," he said and let the bow go slack.

He looked at her properly. She was more dishevelled than he remembered and her face was thinner. Her hair was tangled and snagged with leaves and twigs and her clothes were muddy.

Somewhere nearby a wolf howled suddenly and Erda turned and walked away slowly.

"Stop!" yelled Morgan. "Wait! Come back! You can't leave like this." He plunged down the slope, heedless of the brambles that caught his clothes and the branches that whipped at his face, but by the time he fought his way up the far side of the ravine, Erda was nowhere to be seen.

The wolf howled again, somewhere off to the right. Morgan forced himself to stop and find exactly where she had been standing, looking for any signs to show which way she had gone, but despite sensing that she still held human shape, there was no trail to follow.

He searched for her until darkness threatened to overtake him and he realized he was too far away from the Doors he knew of to get back before nightfall. He had never spent a night in the Underworld and did not relish the prospect as he stood on the straggling edges of a wood with open moorland beyond.

He gathered as much dead wood as he could find — having decided to cut nothing living — and kindled a fire, with every intention of trying to keep it burning through the night. He was so tired. Tomorrow he would go back to Tisian's house to eat and sleep properly or he would be no good to anyone. He settled himself as comfortably as he could against a fallen pine trunk and took a mouthful of his fast-dwindling supply of water, and forced himself to eat a handful of dried fruit although he wasn't hungry.

He meant to stay awake, but he couldn't and was soon walking in the Wildwood with Thomas, both of them half-grown boys again. He woke with a start to find the night half gone and the fire reduced to embers. A full moon hung low in the purple-black sky, yellow as a wolf's eye.

Cursing, he got to his feet and put small sticks onto what was left of his fire, blowing on the embers until they caught light. He added larger branches and as it suddenly flared up he saw Erda sitting with her legs curled under her on the far side of the fire. He leaped

back with an oath, hands scrabbling for a weapon, then
subsided to the ground and stared across at her in
silence.

She leaned forward and stirred the fire with her fingers and he watched in wonder as she withdrew her
hand unharmed from the flames.

"What am I?" she asked him. "You know, don't
you?"

"Yes," he admitted. "You are the Stardreamer."

The fire roared up between them, blocking his view
of her for a few seconds. She was still there when it
subsided.

"What does that mean?" she said. "The words in my
head don't make sense."

"Don't you remember who you are?" he countered.

"I am Erda. I am the Stardreamer. But I do not
know what that means."

It occurred to him as he groped for what to tell her
that she was speaking normally to him. Perhaps he had
imagined it, back at the ravine.

"I know I come from out there," she pointed up at
the night sky, where different stars burned from those
that were visible from the Wildwood, "but none of it
makes sense to me."

"I only know a little," he began. "The Stardreamers
sail in the void until one of them is called down to a
World by those who live there. The Stardreamer has
power ... It can be used by the World."

She'll see into me; see how much I'm not saying, he
thought. *Maybe she can read my thoughts.* But if she
could, she gave no sign of it.

"I still don't understand," she sighed. "Perhaps the
words don't want me to." She stood up and walked a
little way off so that he had half risen to his feet, words
rising unbidden in his throat.

"Don't go."

She came back, dropping to a crouch by the fire, holding her hands up to the flames to warm them. Suddenly she looked him directly in the eye and spoke.

"I am sorry. For what happened to your brother. If I could undo it I would. But I do not have that power. I don't know what to do."

He was about to speak when a sound drew his attention. It came from beyond Erda, just outside the circle of light cast by the fire. He scrambled for his bow, saw her flinch from the corner of his eye.

"Erda! Get over here. There's something out there."

She rose slowly to her feet but made no move to put the fire between her and what moved in the darkness.

Two wolves slipped into the flickering yellow light. For a moment they were all caught in a silent tableau, utterly still, then one of the wolves stretched its neck back and howled and the other sprang at Erda.

Morgan's first shot took it in the flank and his second in the throat. The second wolf sprang and Morgan brought it down with a single shot through the heart.

Erda hadn't moved. She looked now from one silver-furred body to another. Morgan's hands were shaking. He dropped the bow.

"They are coming for you," he said.

She looked at him, smiled and was gone in a swirl of ash.

13. Responsibility

"Kate, what are you doing? It's lunchtime."

"Just coming, mum. I'm on the phone to Sarah."

Kate shut her bedroom door again and carried on the conversation from where it had been interrupted. She and Sarah were trying to arrange a shopping trip to buy something to wear to Jamie Grieve's party the next weekend.

"No, Saturday morning's no good. I told you, I've got football. What about the afternoon?" She listened to Sarah explain why that wasn't possible. "Friday afternoon?" Nope. "It'll have to be today then. Two thirty? Okay. I'll check with the parents and call you back. Bye."

She went into the kitchen. Her parents sat at either end of the table, reading bits of the Sunday paper and eating soup. Ben grinned at her as she sat down opposite him. She reached for a slice of bread.

"What are you so happy about?" she asked, scowling at him.

"You've forgotten, haven't you? Mum, she's forgotten. I told you she had." Ben started to moan.

Oh no, what now?

"Forgotten what?"

Ruth was engrossed in the review section, filtering out the noise of the children's voices as much as possible.

"Mum!" Ben banged his spoon on the table to get her attention.

"Don't do that, Ben," she said, emerging from the paper. "What is it?"

"Kate's forgotten about this afternoon."

"What are you on about? I haven't forgotten anything."

Ruth looked exasperated. "So you're remembering that you'll be looking after Ben this afternoon while your dad and I look at kitchens?"

"What? You never said anything about that. I've just arranged to go shopping with Sarah."

"Well you'd better just un-arrange it then. I told you about this on Wednesday."

"You did not!"

"Of course I did." Ruth held up her hands. "Not another word. That's what's happening."

"That's *so* unfair."

"Do you know that's practically all you say these days?"

"No wonder!" She stomped out of the kitchen, seething.

She wouldn't mind — well, not so much — if she'd heard anything about this before, but she was sure she hadn't. *Fairly* sure. She called Sarah to cancel and listened to predictions of the ridicule they would face when they didn't have the right stuff for the party. She stayed mutinously in her room until she heard her parents getting ready to go out, then emerged so that she could stand around looking glum.

Ruth steadfastly ignored her expression, instead giving her a list of instructions of what to do and when they would be back. As they went out the front door her dad handed her some money.

"Thanks, love. That's to buy the pair of you an ice cream. I'll try and make it quick. Maybe you can meet Sarah after we come back."

"I don't think so, but thanks, Dad."

As soon as the door had shut, Ben said, "Is that ice cream money?"

"Yes, maggot, and you don't deserve any."

"That's not fair. I'll tell."

She gave a theatrical sigh. "Believe me, I know. Don't worry you little rat, you'll get your ice cream, though you don't deserve it."

"Can we go and play football on the Links first?"

"I suppose so. Go on then, find a ball."

Actually, once they were out it wasn't too bad. It was warm and sunny again and some of Ben's friends were there already so they soon got a game going. She ran rings around them for a bit then got bored and went to sit on a bench and watch. A couple of her own friends wandered past, en route to town to mooch around Princes Street Gardens, and they stopped to chat for a while. When they'd gone she tried calling David, but his phone was switched off. She left a message anyway, in case he looked at it soon.

The football game was breaking up, small boys heading off in various directions.

"Come on, Ben," she called. "Ice cream time."

He gave a whoop, retrieved his ball and ran across to the bench where she sat.

"Can we go to Luca's? Please? I know Dad gave you enough money."

"Oh, all right." She tried to look long-suffering, though in fact she had been about to suggest it herself. Luca's was a legendary Italian ice cream shop. When she was little the family had made pilgrimages by car all the way to neighbouring Musselburgh to wait in long queues for Strawberry 99s, but now they had a shop barely ten minutes walk from home, and they'd discovered that the ice cream tasted just as good even if you hadn't sat sweltering in a traffic jam to get to it.

When they got there they ignored the new-fangled delights of the Irn Bru Sorbet and other exotic flavours and opted for classic Strawberry in the largest size their money would buy.

They dawdled back in silence, savouring the flavour of the summer yet to come, licking drips off their hands, intent on consuming every morsel.

By the time they got back to the Links, Kate had finished hers and a fair proportion of Ben's was spread around his mouth. As they waited to cross the road Kate looked idly at the people walking over the grass; no footballers at the moment, in fact, no one she knew.

Her heart skipped a beat, for there was Erda, stepping suddenly from behind a tree. She looked terrible, unkempt and dirty, her hair a tangled mess. She'd lost weight even in the few days since Kate had last seen her. At that moment she didn't think at all about the fact that Erda was supposedly the Stardreamer, this powerful being. She was simply Erda: lost, lonely and scarcely capable of looking after herself.

"Erda!" she called.

Erda looked up and saw her and a strange expression passed across her face. She seemed undecided whether to come over or turn and walk away.

As she hesitated, Kate yelled, "Stay here!" to Ben and ran across the road, dodging cars, ignoring his cries of "Kate! Come back!" She had almost reached Erda when she saw the expression on her face change as she focused on something happening behind Kate.

The world seemed to slow down.

Kate heard a terrible sound, a screeching of brakes, then someone screamed and she turned, infinitely slowly and saw Ben lying on the road in front of a blue car, the ice cream smashed on the tarmac beside him.

"Ben!" she screamed and ran. By the time she had covered the fifty metres that separated them, the white-faced driver had climbed from the car and a small crowd had gathered. Someone was phoning for an ambulance.

She heard someone screaming, "Let me past, it's my brother," and realized it was her. Then she was sitting on the ground beside Ben. He lay quite still, his eyes shut.

"Ben, Ben wake up," she said desperately over and over, but he didn't.

Kate heard her parents before she saw them.

"Excuse me — we had a phone call. My son was brought in. He's been knocked down by a car ..." Mum's voice, breaking, trailing off, then Dad, "His name's Ben Dalgliesh. His sister was with him when he was brought in."

The nurse who had been sitting with her got up.

"I'll just take them in to see him for a minute, then I'll bring them in here, love." Kate nodded dumbly.

Five minutes passed, then ten. It was almost fifteen before Mum and Dad come into the room where she sat alone, a doctor with them. They both looked as if they'd been crying.

"I thought I'd explain things to you all together," said the doctor as she sat down. "Ben's awake now and he's going to be fine. He's a very lucky boy: no broken bones, just cuts and bruises and mild concussion. The car must hardly have been moving when it hit him. We'll keep him in overnight for observation just to make sure everything's fine and he can go home in the morning." She smiled at them sympathetically. "You've all had a shock, but really there's no need to worry. Kids get worse knocks than this in the playground every day. I'll leave you in peace for a while here, then get someone to bring you some tea."

She went out, shutting the door behind her and

Kate heard her mother draw a deep breath.

"What happened, Kate?" asked her dad gently. This was what she'd been dreading since she found out that Ben was okay.

"It was my fault," she mumbled.

"I'm sure it wasn't," said Dad. 'Just tell us what happened.'

"I saw someone I knew on the Links and ran across the road to speak to them. I told Ben to stay where he was but he must have run after me and then ..." Her voice trailed away.

"Oh, Kate, how could you?" Her mother's voice was quiet. It would have been better if she'd shouted, Kate thought dully.

"I'm sorry," she whispered.

"He could have been killed. You were supposed to be looking after him."

"Now, Ruth ..." Robert put a hand on his wife's arm. "You're upset, we all are. Don't ..."

Kate couldn't fight the tears back any more. "I know it's my fault. I'm sorry. I wish the car had hit me instead," she sobbed and ran out of the room, out of the hospital, away.

Alastair took the phone call just before nine that evening. "No, she's not here ... Oh my God, is he all right? I'll check with David ... yes, of course; I'll let you know right away."

David had looked up at the mention of his name and so he saw the look on Alastair's face as he came into the room.

"What is it, Dad? What's wrong?"

"Kate's disappeared. She was looking after Ben this afternoon and he was knocked down by a car. He's okay, but Kate got very upset at the hospital and ran away. They thought she might be here. You haven't heard from her, have you?"

"No." David was aghast. "Wait a minute and I'll check my phone. I think I switched it off."

He went to his bedroom and brought the phone back.

"She tried to call me just before three."

"No. That's before it happened, I think. Have you any idea where she might have gone? They've tried all her friends — they couldn't get us before because I was on the computer."

He had of course, but he could hardly say where. He shook his head. Alastair went out of the room to tell Christine what had happened.

David gave it five minutes, then went to speak to his dad.

"Can I go out and look around for her? I've had a couple of ideas."

"I'll come with you."

"No!" said David, too quickly. Alastair looked at him suspiciously. "Please, Dad, let me go on my own. I know what I'm doing. I'll take my phone."

"All right, but don't do anything stupid, will you? And be back by ten whether you've found her or not."

"I will. Thanks, Dad."

He shut the front door behind him, walked to the corner and as soon as he was out of sight of the window from which he was sure his father would be watching, tore down the street as fast as he could.

It took him barely five minutes to reach the house, panting for breath. He'd seen no lights as he ran down the hill towards it. Now he fumbled for the key, dropped it, picked it up and opened the door to the dark hallway. He switched on the light and looked around for any sign that Kate was here, but there was nothing.

"Kate!" he shouted. "Are you here?"

Nothing. The house seemed extra quiet, as though it was holding its breath. He moved through it, checking each room as he went. The house seemed quite empty. He poked his head round the door of the little bedroom which held the Door to Tisian's house. What if she had run through there?

When he went up to the second floor he was trying to decide whether to try and go through the Door himself in case she was there. He pushed open the door to the study, saw the humped silhouettes of the furniture in the faint wash of moonlight from the window and switched on the light.

Kate was curled in the big old armchair, fast asleep. He could see from her face she must have cried herself to sleep.

For a moment, he couldn't think what to do. Should he phone someone or wake her? The cold little part of his brain that watched things without becoming involved said, *Don't phone. How will you explain the keys? You'll never be able to come back.* It was right. Anyway, he'd be just as quick waking her and taking her home as phoning and waiting for someone to come.

He crouched down beside the chair.

"Kate?" There was no response. "Come on, Kate. Time to wake up." He shook her gently by the shoulder and she stirred and stretched and opened her eyes and he saw in them the instant in which she remembered what had happened.

She stared at him. "You know what happened, don't you?"

He nodded. "Ben's okay. Your parents are really worried about you. They've been phoning everyone, trying to find you." He stood up and held out a hand to her. "Come on. I'll walk home with you."

She didn't move. "It was my fault, you know. I saw Erda and I left Ben by the road and ran off to talk to her, and he ran after me. I shouldn't have left him, it's my fault."

"You weren't to know he'd run after you. You shouldn't blame yourself."

"My mother does. She's right. I've been thinking about that letter — what it said about the Darkness inside us — maybe that's why I did it. Maybe I'm like *them.*"

David was taken aback. "Kate, that's nuts! This was nothing to do with the Lords of Chaos; it was an accident."

"Maybe I wanted it to happen, so it did."

David tried to keep calm. "You're upset, you're tired. Come on, let's go home. It'll be better tomorrow." He held out his hand and this time she took it and got slowly up.

He locked the front door behind them and they set off up the hill. Kate walked with her arms wrapped round her, sunk deep in misery. David wanted to put an arm round her to comfort her, but she was too remote, locked somewhere far away in her head.

They reached her house. David paused before ringing the bell at the bottom of the stairs, the cold little part of him in charge again.

"Kate, where are we going to say I found you?"

She shrugged. "I don't know."

He thought. "Just say you were walking around all the time and I found you near the school. All right?"

She nodded and he rang the bell.

"Yes?"

"It's David. I've got Kate with me."

"Oh, thank God." The buzzer sounded and he pushed the door open.

Kate's mum was already halfway down the stairs. She engulfed Kate in a tight hug, tears running down her face.

"Kate, where have you been? We've been so worried. I'm sorry about what I said at the hospital. I'm so sorry ..."

David turned and left quietly and walked slowly home.

14. Choices

Tethys howled with fury as she looked at the corpses of the wolves.

"I will have his heart for this," she shrieked. So agitated had she become that the physical form she usually wore was blurred and twisting at the edges, like a figure seen through a heat haze, giving glimpses of what lay beneath.

The Hunter gave a short laugh and she stilled immediately.

"You set your pets to hunt often enough without a thought for the quarry," he said. "Perhaps this is what they mean when they talk of justice." The thought seemed to please him and he laughed again.

Tethys gave him a look that burned with resentment, but her voice, when she spoke again, had grown quiet. "I claim his life for what he has done."

"You will not touch him." The Hunter's voice was calm, but as she spoke he had moved in a heartbeat to where she stood and twisting his hand into her dripping hair, forced her head back. He traced her throat with a filthy nail and though she stood still, her form was frayed at the edges again. "You will not touch him. We need him and when we do not, he is mine. If you touch him I will feed you to my hounds."

The Queen watched the exchange eagerly, feeding on the conflict.

"Does it matter if he destroys her?" asked the Lightning King softly, lounging at her side.

"Not now," she replied. "Better that than that she should destroy Morgan. He is our best chance to control the Stardreamer if we cannot do it through the children."

The Hunter let Tethys go. She sprang back, hissing like a cat, and fled.

"Where have you been, while Morgan has been killing poor Tethys' wolves?" The Queen plucked a tendril of lightning from the King's robe and watched it twist.

"I believe I have found us a gateway into the children's world," he replied. "It only remains for someone to invite us to step through it. The barriers there are so thin almost anyone will do ..."

Kate wasn't at school the next day. David was distracted in classes, fretting about her, then feeling guilty for not being more worried about Ben. He tried calling and texting her, but could see that visitors might be unwelcome just now.

On the off chance that she might be there — though he would have been surprised if she was — he walked down to the house after school. There was no trace of Kate, but Erda was there, as though she'd never been away, sitting on the kitchen table, eating cereal from the packet.

They stared at each other in silence, Erda with a handful halfway to her mouth.

"Where have you been? We were worried about you." He took in her appearance, torn, filthy and drawn. "You look terrible. What happened to you?" He knew all too well, of course, but wanted to see what she would say.

She turned the question aside. "Kate's brother was hurt," she said, "but he will be better?" It was half-statement, half-question.

"Yes."

"But what about Kate? Her spirit is hurt by what happened. Where is she? I cannot see her. She is trying not to be."

"She thinks it was her fault."

Erda looked distressed. "No! It was my fault — this as well." She sighed, pushing her tangled hair back from her face.

"Maybe I can bring her to talk to you and you can convince her it wasn't her fault," he suggested. "Promise you won't run away again anyway."

"Promise?" She looked puzzled. There was no picture in her mind.

He tried to think of a way to explain it, but as he did so he saw comprehension spread over her face.

"Ah … promise. I understand. I will try."

Well, it was half a promise. Now all he had to do was get Kate.

To his surprise, she called soon after he got home, asking him to go round to her house later. He felt very unsure as he rang the doorbell. He must have stood here like this hundreds of times, but tonight he didn't know what to expect.

Kate opened the door. She looked okay, maybe a bit pale, or maybe he was imagining it.

"Mum and Dad want to say hello and Ben wants to show off his bruises," she said with a wry smile. "You may as well get it over with now."

They went into the sitting room and Ruth immediately got up and came over to hug David, much to his embarrassment.

"David, thank you so much for yesterday. You've been such a good friend to Kate …" Robert contented himself with nodding in agreement from the sofa, while Ben sniggered at David's discomfort from behind his mother's back.

"Look at my bruises!" he yelled a few seconds later.

David had to admit he looked quite impressive, one

side of his face — he insisted on showing David his matching body as well — was blotted with scrapes and patches of blue and purple, with a line of paper stitches above one eyebrow where he had cut his head.

He was just as annoying as usual though; if you shut your eyes, everything was completely normal.

As soon as it became possible, Kate and David extracted themselves and took refuge in Kate's bedroom.

"So," David said, "I've seen Ben's bruises; how are *you*?"

"Okay." She gave a shaky smile. "I keep seeing it happen if I'm not concentrating on something else. The doctor said that's normal and it'll go away, but ..." She sought for words. "You know, it sort of creeps up on me ..." She shook her head as if to clear the vision from it.

"Thanks for last night," she went on. "I was in such a state I didn't know what to do. I thought Mum and Dad would hate me for what happened ... I couldn't go home.

"They're being really nice about it, but it was my fault. Ben could have been killed."

"But he wasn't. He's fine. Anyway, Erda says it was her fault, not yours."

Kate frowned. "When did you talk to her?"

"After school. She's back at the house. She wants to see you. She wants to convince you that she's to blame, not you. We could go round tomorrow."

Kate looked away suddenly.

"I don't know ... All this stuff Mr Flowerdew said about the Light and Darkness in us — maybe what happened with Ben was the Darkness coming out."

"Kate, no!" David interrupted. "It was an accident — a straightforward accident. Ben ran into the road."

"But it wouldn't have happened if I hadn't seen Erda. If I was leading a normal life, like everyone else. That's what I want David, I want to be like everyone else; I don't want to come and see Erda, I want all that to stop."

David bit back the words that threatened to spill out and tried to keep his voice level. 'We are what we are, Kate. Pretending won't change it."

"But didn't Mr Flowerdew say in that letter 'Do what you think is right?'"

"Yes, but ..."

"This is what I think is right. I'm not having anything else to do with Lords or Guardians or Stardreamers. I've got a family and friends here and now, they're more important."

David thought fast. "You're right. It's your decision; but *please* just come and say goodbye to Erda tomorrow. She feels so guilty about what's happened.

"You know what that feels like," he added, turning the knife ruthlessly.

Kate closed her eyes briefly, then gave a resigned sigh. "Promise that if I come you'll leave me out of all this afterwards?"

"Promise," lied David.

"'All right. I'll come."

They discussed football on the way. All the school teams, boys and girls, were playing in a tournament against the equivalent teams from their great rivals, one of the other local schools, the next weekend.

"They're terrible hackers," said Kate.

"*And* they're always taking dives," David added. "We'll probably all lose."

"Brian'll go spare if we lose again." Brian was the long-suffering coach of the team Kate played for; one of the dads who inexplicably gave up their Saturday mornings week after week, for no other reward than sometimes seeing their players triumph.

"George won't be too pleased either. We've lost our last

three matches." George was the coach for David's team and seemed to take every defeat as a personal blow.

They pushed the gate open.

"Are you sure she's going to be here?"

"No. I hope she is. She said she'd stay."

Kate opened the door and David called Erda's name. She came down the stairs. She looked better than she had yesterday, David thought. She'd combed her hair and looked as though she'd had some sleep and she'd changed into cleaner clothes. She looked apprehensive as she approached Kate.

"I am sorry your brother was hurt. It was my fault. You would not have left him if I had not been there." Kate opened her mouth to protest, but Erda went on, "Your brother will be better soon. He is not much hurt." She put a hand up to Kate's cheek. "You think it is you who made this happen, but it is not. It is nothing inside you. You have done nothing wrong."

Kate gaped at her, astonished. How could she know what Kate was thinking, feeling? Kate spoke. "You too. You should stop blaming yourself for Ben and for Thomas. We know what happened. It was an accident. Even Morgan understands that now. Stop running from him. Let him help you."

Erda shook her head. "I have caused someone's death. That will not go away." She looked up. "I must go. He is coming."

"What? Morgan is coming?" Kate looked round, wondering if that was what Erda meant. When she turned back, Erda was gone. "Erda? David, where did she go?"

David looked blank. "I don't know. She just ... wasn't there suddenly. I don't understand."

They ran to the door and went out into the street, but she was nowhere to be seen. They came back inside, baffled.

Morgan was coming down the stairs. The look on their faces told him. "She was here, wasn't she? I've missed her again."

There was a bow in his hand, a fact of which he seemed quite unconscious. Kate looked at it nervously.

"Why do you need that?"

He noticed it and sat down a couple of steps from the bottom, laying it carefully down beside him. "I'm sorry. I forgot I had it with me when I came through the Door." He stopped to read their expressions again. "I'm not hunting her. Not like that. It's for protection. I think something hunts us both."

He had spent two days with Tisian after killing the wolves, resting and talking and speculating, and she had told him about the children's visit.

"I know you spoke to Tisian. I know what she told you."

"Why did you lie to us before?" asked Kate suspiciously.

Morgan sighed. "It was easier. You seemed to be her friends. You would never have helped me if you had known what I meant to do."

"Why do you assume we wouldn't have understood if you had explained it properly?" demanded David.

"You are young." Morgan was taken aback by the question. "You are barely more than children."

"You don't know anything about us," said David angrily. "We have fought for the Guardians. We faced the Water Witch and the Lightning King. We understand much more than you think."

"I am sorry. You are right. I should not underestimate you because you are so young." He got to his feet and propped the bow against the wall. "I must go after Erda. I'll leave this here."

"Why?" said Kate suddenly.

"No one carries them in your ..."

"Not the bow," Kate cut him off. "Why do you have to go after Erda?"

So much for understanding.

"Now that the Stardreamer's power has been brought to the Worlds it must be merged with the Heart of the Earth. If the Lords have their way and her power is released outside, all that we know will be destroyed."

"Why can't you just let her go?"

"Go?"

"Yes. Go back to the stars, space, wherever it is. The power would be removed and the Worlds would be safe. She didn't ask to come here. It's not right. You're all trying to use her."

Morgan stared at the girl in astonishment. For the moment he couldn't think of an answer, of a reason why she was wrong, but she must be wrong, surely?

"You should ask her what she wants when you do find her. Maybe she wants to be left alone."

David was avidly watching the change of expression on Morgan's face. He looked completely baffled, as if all the certainties of life had just been taken from him.

"Whatever happens, I have to find her," he said, and pushed past them out of the front door.

David turned to Kate. "Wow! That was quite something. I wish I'd thought of that. Did you see his face?"

Kate fished in her pocket, pulled out her keys to Mr Flowerdew's house and put them down on the table beside the grandfather clock.

"Kate, what are you doing?" asked David, a chill creeping through him.

Kate's face was serious. "I'm not coming back here. I told you, David, I'm done with all this. I don't want to be a Child of Light and Darkness. I want to be normal." She opened the front door. "See you at school tomorrow."

And she was gone.

15. Rosslyn

It was very weird. Kate was at school the next day, acting as if nothing had happened, answering questions about Ben's accident without getting upset; being *normal*. Being determinedly normal.

They sat together in the lessons they shared as usual and chatted away and all the time David was thinking *Come on, Kate. See sense. You can't keep this up.*

But she did.

They walked part of the way home together and when they came to the point at which the routes to Kate's and Mr Flowerdew's houses diverged, she said goodbye and turned towards her home without hesitation.

David found he didn't want to go on his own just then, so he turned and trudged home, unable to decide whether to be irritated or worried.

"I'm back," he shouted to Claire as he came in and heard a muffled reply from the kitchen. He dropped his bag and sweatshirt. No Tiger to wind himself, purring, round his legs. There was a delicious smell when he opened the kitchen door.

"Mmmn, that smells good," he said as he went to make himself a sandwich.

"It's just a chicken roasting," said Claire absently, peering at the calendar. "Even you could make it. Half a lemon up its bum and Bob's your uncle."

"Charming. That's put me right off it."

"You won't be saying that when it's on a plate in front of you though.

"What age are you now?"

He did a double take. "I'm thirteen. You know I'm thirteen. Why?"

"It's about time you learned to cook."

"I *can* cook."

"I don't mean putting pizza in the oven. Proper food."

"Like roast chicken?"

"Like roast chicken. I'm not always going to be able to cook your tea for you, you know."

David's blood ran cold. Christine must have done it. She must have told Claire to leave.

"She can't make you leave. Don't listen to her. You mustn't go."

"Leave? What are you talking about? I'm not leaving. I'm talking about when the baby comes."

David was flabbergasted. "You're having a baby?"

Claire closed her eyes and put her hands briefly over her face.

"Oh dear, Davie boy." She took her hands away. "Not me, you eejit. I thought you knew."

David could feel his mouth hanging open, but he couldn't summon the will to shut it.

"Christine's having a baby. The last thing she wants is for me to leave. She wants me to look after it."

"Oh." It was a stupid response, but it seemed to be the only sound he could make.

"Let me guess. Christine tried to tell you and you jumped to the wrong conclusion?"

He replayed *that* conversation in his head and nodded.

Claire sighed and sat down opposite David at the table.

"I know it's hard for you, but it's hard for her too. You need to give her more of a chance, listen to her properly instead of leaping to conclusions whenever she opens her mouth."

A baby. A little brother or sister. Like Ben. He burst out laughing at the thought.

"All right. Next time they try to tell you, *listen*. And for goodness sake act surprised. You shouldn't have been hearing this from me at all."

A baby. He nodded. "Trust me. I'm good at surprised. Now, what do you do to the chicken once you've stuck the melon up its bum?"

Claire threw a tea towel at him and they both dissolved into laughter.

The next couple of days were uneventful enough to satisfy even Kate. David told her about the baby, about whose existence he'd managed to get himself told the same evening he'd had the conversation with Claire.

She beamed.

"David, that's great. A baby, wow."

"You never say Ben's great."

"That's different. He's a maggot, not a baby. So are things okay with you and Christine then?"

He thought of the fragile truce between the two of them, through which they were tiptoeing as though the slightest mistake might shatter it — which it might, of course.

"Yeah, sort of."

"Kate, David; less talk and more drawing please."

"Sorry Miss."

It was double Art, one of David's favourites.

"Don't forget the Art Club trip on Monday," Miss Roberts said to the class.

"What time do we get back?" someone asked.

"It was all on the consent form," Miss Roberts said with a sigh. "Don't you ever read them? No, don't bother answering.

"We leave at three — you'll have to get permission to miss last lesson. We're going in the minibus. We'll be back at five thirty. Got that?"

"Are there any spare places?" asked Kate.

"There might be. I'll check." Miss Roberts retreated to her desk.

"I thought you didn't want to join the Art Club?" said David.

"I don't, but Mum keeps going on about this Chapel place, says I ought to go and see it, so I thought I would."

"There is a place Kate," called Miss Roberts. "Do you want me to put you down?"

"Yes please."

"You'll need to take this form home and get it signed."

"Okay, thanks."

David tried again on the way home that day. "Do you want to come round to the house for a while? At least to water the plants?"

Kate shook her head. "I'm sure you can manage. I've got a Chemistry test tomorrow. I want to try and do better this time."

"Oh. All right. See you tomorrow then."

"Bye."

He decided he'd better go and look at the plants. They kept forgetting to do them, with everything that had been happening. He didn't know if he wanted to see Morgan and Erda, but in the event neither of them was there, so he topped up the plant pots and went home.

Monday afternoon came: end of school, sun and blue sky yet again and the same forecast for the next few days. Twelve of them jostled for the best places on the minibus while Miss Roberts and Mr Graham got in the front more sedately, carrying bags of art material.

"Put your seatbelts on."

It was still early enough that the roads weren't clogged with people escaping home from work for the day.

"The famous Rosslyn Chapel," said Mr Graham as they got out of the bus.

They could only see the top half of the Chapel from where they were, their view blocked by a wall and the visitors' centre.

Kate squinted up into the light. The Chapel was shrouded in scaffolding. Behind the metal poles and walkways she could make out pinnacles of dark grey and honey-coloured stone. They milled about the shop, picking things up and putting them down, while the teachers paid the entry fee, then they emerged from a door to find themselves on the other side of the wall.

"Right everyone. We'll have a walk round the out-side first. It looks as though we can get up on the scaffolding, there are steps and a walkway, look, there.

"Once we've done that we'll go in and have a look at some of the carvings I've been telling you about, then you can spread out and choose where to work. Remember you're in a church though: behave properly."

They walked together round the base of the Chapel, pausing to look at an ornate tomb and at a crumbling carving of a dove eating fruit, then climbed the clang-ing metal stairs up to the scaffold walkway. It went all the way round the Chapel and though some of their friends decided to have a race round it, Kate and David dawdled to look out over the countryside.

To the east there was a steep, wooded valley, from which came the sound of running water. They walked further round and looked out to the south. Over the wall which surrounded the Chapel grounds in this direction lay scrubby ground, except in one place, where there was a little meadow of parched grass on which half a dozen rabbits hopped, unconcerned. They watched the white scuts bouncing up and down.

"Look, Kate." David pointed to one edge of the meadow. Kate looked and saw a black rabbit.

"Wow," she breathed. 'Have you ever seen one like that?'

"No," whispered David. Their classmates appeared below them, laughing and talking, but the rabbit, oblivious to their presence, hopped into the centre of the grass as they watched, mesmerized.

"Kate! David! Come on down. We're going inside now."

The spell was broken. The rabbits looked up sharply and disappeared in a multiple flash of white and they went down to join the others.

The cold struck Kate as soon as she crossed the threshold. It raced up from the stone through her body and she shivered. Beside her David rubbed his arms and stamped his feet.

"It's freezing in here," he said.

Miss Roberts laughed. "It's just that you've been out in the sun. It's always cool in here because of how thick the stone is — you should try coming here in winter; it feels colder inside than out, even when there's snow on the ground — but it's not *that* cold today."

Right enough, no one else seemed to feel it, standing unconcerned and un-goosepimpled in their tee-shirts.

They moved slowly round the Chapel listening as Miss Roberts and Mr Graham pointed out details of the carvings: Robert the Bruce's heart, a fallen angel bound with ropes, sweetcorn and bagpipes and the dance of death and, of course, the Prentice Pillar, gorgeously carved by a disobedient apprentice in his master's absence; the 'prentice supposedly murdered by the master mason on his return. And everywhere, over and over again, the strange figure of the Green Man — not fit for a Christian church at all, said Mr Graham — a face with vines emerging from its mouth, not a comfortable thing to have looking down at you, thought Kate. She shivered again, not just from the cold.

They were given pencils, paper and drawing boards and set loose. David tried first to draw some of the carving from the pillar, but it was too complicated. He settled down instead to draw some of the angels, wishing he'd had the sense to bring a sweatshirt with him.

It took Kate longer to settle. She wandered around looking at the visitors' book, reading notices, trying to get warm. Finally she started drawing the carved vine which seemed to go all the way round the Chapel, but her fingers were too cold to hold the pencil properly.

"Hey, Kate, come and see what I've found."

Kate looked round to see Jamie Grieve. "What?" she asked suspiciously, wary of a trick.

"There's a downstairs bit they didn't show us — a crypt or something. Come on down and have a look."

"All right — just for a minute," she said cautiously.

He led her to the end of the Chapel where David was working, persuading another two classmates on the way.

"David," Kate tugged at his sleeve.

"What?"

"Jamie wants me to go and look at something with him. I bet it's a trick. Come with me?"

"Sure." He put down his drawing.

Jamie stood at the top of a short flight of steps they'd thought was closed off from the public, but now that they looked properly, they could see it wasn't. It led down, not into the creepy darkness Kate had expected, but to a brightly lit room, much smaller than

the Chapel above, with a ceiling curved like the inside
of a barrel and a stained glass window at one end. It
was even colder down here.

Despite the presence of a big stone with a figure of
Death carved on it, it wasn't really very interesting.
They looked at the information boards without taking
in the information. Kate glanced up at David. He was
pale and frowning.

"Are you okay?"

"My head hurts. I think I'll go outside for a bit."

"Wow! Look at this." Jamie's voice sounded genuinely excited. He'd pushed open a door and found
another little room. In it stood an enormous cupboard,
made of wood that was almost black, covered in carvings of knights and coats of arms and what looked like
a scene from the garden of Eden. It looked as if it had
stood there forever.

It was so cold in the room that Kate's head had
begun to ache. She couldn't understand why it didn't
seem to be affecting anyone else.

Except David. Oh no. What was going on?

"I wonder what's in it?" Jamie was saying. She
watched his hand reach out to turn the key and found
herself yelling, "No! Don't open it!"

Jamie paused, laughing. "Why, Kate? Afraid the
Bogeyman's in there?"

No. Something much worse.

She felt David's hand on her arm. Jamie turned the
key and pulled open the black door.

16. The Invitation

There was utter silence for a few seconds, then Kate let out the breath she hadn't realized she was holding and Jamie burst out laughing at her.

'You should see your face. What on earth were you expecting to happen?'

David and Kate looked at the contents of the cupboard: a jumble of mops and buckets and dusters.

"Ha ha. Very funny." She pushed her way out of the door and stood pretending to read an information board, her heart still hammering unpleasantly, her head pounding in time with her heart beats. David joined her a few seconds later.

"Ignore him, Kate. Everyone knows he's an idiot."

They could hear Jamie, still in the room with the cupboard, imitating Kate in a stupid falsetto voice. "No! Don't open it. The Bogeyman might be in there."

"Let's go in here." David pointed to another doorway opposite the cupboard room. "Maybe there's something in it we can use to get our own back."

It didn't look promising. It was dimly lit, certainly, but there was nowhere you could hide to jump out on someone. All it held were slatted shelves with bits of masonry displayed on them, and a smallish window with no glass, but a wooden shutter with holes in it, through which narrow beams of sunlight shone on the dusty stones. Kate went over to it and peered out. There was an iron grille on the outside, and beyond it the window looked straight onto a grassy slope. Although it was just the right height for Kate to look out of, from the outside it must only be a foot or so off the ground.

The cold had become intolerable.

"Come on, let's go," said Kate, but as she did so Jamie and his mates pushed past.

"Hiding Kate? Or planning your revenge?" he said, doing a Frankenstein walk across to the window. He peered out of one of the peepholes and jumped back with a yelp.

In spite of herself Kate jumped.

"You're pathetic, Jamie," she said in disgust.

"No. I got a fright. There's someone outside the window. I wasn't expecting it. Honest. Come and see." He put his eye back to the peephole.

Kate moved to the window as though the air was as thick as honey, David at her side. She knew it was ridiculous, but she was terribly afraid, even though she could hear Jamie having a perfectly normal conversation with the person on the other side of the shutter.

"Yes, we're on a school trip. Drawing." Something the other person said made him smile.

Kate had reached the shutter. She put her eye to one of the holes and looked out, full of dread. A woman's face looked back at her, lit by a friendly smile. Impossible: the window was almost at ground level. No one could stand and look into it like that.

"Hello. Are you with the school trip too? Your friend's been telling me about all your drawings. I'd love to see some of them." She paused. "It's very difficult having a conversation like this. Why don't you open the shutter?"

Kate wanted to yell, tried to make a sound and found she couldn't.

"All right," she heard Jamie say. "Hang on."

Beside her she could see David struggling to move or speak.

"Oh — here it is. There's a bolt. Just a minute — it's stiff."

Kate summoned every particle of strength she had and shouted "Jamie! Don't!" and heard it come out as a whisper.

Jamie paused to look at her curiously. "What are you on about now, Kate?"

She felt David grab her arm and pull her back from the window with horrible slowness as the bolt finally yielded to Jamie's efforts and he swung the shutter back against the wall.

Framed head and shoulders was a woman with long twisting black hair and milk-pale skin. What was visible of her clothes was a dark, rusty red. She smiled at them all through the iron grille.

"Aren't you going to invite me in?"

"No!" whispered Kate and David as loudly as they could, still backing away.

For a second she seemed to waver in the air, but then she turned the light of her smile on Jamie and he spoke, his eyes never leaving her face. "Of course. Come in."

And somehow she was in the room with them. She turned her terrible smile on Kate and David. "I have waited a long time to meet you two face to face."

Whatever spell had held them broke.

"Run!" yelled David and they turned and scrambled for the stairs, up into the blinding light of the Chapel and out into the sunlight.

They stood on the path outside the Chapel door, panting and shaking, each seeing the fear they felt reflected in the other's eyes.

"What happened in there? Who — *what* was that?" gabbled Kate. "It was one of *them* wasn't it? One of the Lords of Chaos?"

David nodded, trying to get his breath back.

"We have to tell someone — warn them."

"Yes. Right,' said David, then stopped. 'Does that mean going back inside?"

They looked at each other, then began to edge back up the path towards the door, ready to run again if the woman appeared, but they didn't get far. Miss Roberts appeared in the doorway, looking furious and came straight towards them.

"What on earth do you think you're doing? I told you to behave. This is a *church* you know. Honestly, I expected better of you two."

"But Miss Roberts, Jamie let someone in through a window down in the basement place and ..." Kate's voice trailed away as she realized how pathetic she sounded.

Just then Jamie and his friends appeared in the doorway.

"What have you been doing, Jamie?"

He looked genuinely puzzled, as did the others. "Me? Nothing. I've just been drawing like you said."

"What's this about you messing about with a window down in the basement?"

"A *window*? I don't know what you're talking about." If he was acting, it was very convincing.

"Kate?" Miss Roberts turned a cold look on her.

"I ... I'm sorry, Miss. I ... must have made a mistake."

"Whatever's been going on, that's quite enough. Go and get your things and wait in the bus."

"Yes Miss."

They watched glumly as the others went back into the Chapel and forced themselves to follow them and collect their abandoned drawing things. There was no sign of the woman Jamie had let in.

Kate shuddered. "Let's get away from here."

They made their way back out through the visitors'

centre and climbed into the unlocked bus, where they
huddled in the back seat, looking nervously around for
the thing that they had seen.

"We have to warn Morgan and Erda. The Lords of
Chaos must be coming for her," said David. For a
moment Kate didn't reply and he could tell that she
was wrestling with her feelings. "Kate?" he said gently.

"I know, I know. They've broken through into our
world somehow. That's something Mr Flowerdew said
couldn't happen, but it has. There's no use me pretending this isn't happening or that it's nothing to do
with me. *She* knew who we were — whoever she was —
and she knew that we would recognize her for what
she was. I know I have to try and help; but what if *they*
try to make us do something to help them, like they did
last time."

"But we *didn't* help them last time, even though
they tried.' David's face had gone remote, as he
remembered what he had let go on the shores of
Duddingston Loch eighteen months before.

"But we didn't know then ...*what we are*. Part of us
is like them. Something of them is in us."

"But we're the same people we were before we read
that letter," David almost yelled.

"Are we? I don't feel as if I'm the same. I feel as if
I'm ... dangerous. I don't trust myself any more."

David didn't know what to say. He couldn't think of
anything that would convince Kate. They were stuck
in this bus and there was nothing either of them could
do to warn Morgan or Erda until they got back to
Edinburgh.

As soon as they got off the bus back at school and were
out of earshot of other people, they each phoned home
and said they'd been invited to tea by the other, then

they raced to the house to try and warn Morgan and
Erda. They knew as soon as they opened the door that
it was deserted, but they checked all the rooms anyway.

"They could be anywhere. What do we do? How can
we find them?" Kate was half frantic. "Tisian! We have
to use the Door. She might know where Morgan is, or
what we should do."

They took the stairs two at a time and raced into the
little spare bedroom, shoved the door closed and pulled
it open again straight away.

Corridor and stairs.

They tried again, closing the door more gently and
counting to ten before they opened it.

Corridor and stairs.

Again. Wait for a whole minute with the door shut.

Again. Five minutes.

Again.

Again.

Again.

They tried to visualize the patchwork hanging that
concealed the Door in Tisian's world, opened their door
with their eyes shut, reached out to touch the cloth ...

Corridor and stairs.

They sat side by side on the narrow single bed.

"Think," said Kate. "What did we do to open the
Door last time?"

"Nothing. Nothing I can remember anyway." He got
up and opened the door to the corridor again. In front
of him hung a patchwork.

They had never truly set foot in the Wildwood when
they came through the Door before, but as soon as they
were sure Tisian wasn't in her house, they went outside.

The wood hung about them, ancient, mossy, glossed
with dew. Sun slanted through the branches. It seemed

to be early morning. They'd been in woods before of course, but nothing like this. It was sharper, more vivid, more *real* somehow, than anywhere they had ever been. Even the air had flavour. For precious minutes they stood dumbstruck in the clearing around Tisian's house. It was not quiet. There was a constant ripple of sound: leaves sliding their palms together, branches creaking, water, birds; you could almost hear the place breathe.

"No wonder he wants to save it," said Kate quietly.

"There's a path here," said David. "Let's see where it goes."

"What if we get lost? This wood looks as though it goes on for miles."

"We'll stay on the path."

They walked for perhaps twenty minutes, trees stretching away to uncertainty on either side of them. They heard birds in the branches above their heads without ever seeing them, but once they caught sight of a black rabbit disappearing into a tangle of pink-blossomed brambles, then voices came to them carried on the breeze and they quickened their pace.

Tisian and Morgan stood together deep in conversation near a rowan tree with a recently dug patch of earth by its roots. Morgan must have heard them, for he looked up and seeing their faces, ran to meet them.

Words tumbled out of them both at once, incomprehensible. Morgan held up a hand.

"Slowly, slowly."

"Sit down," added Tisian, arriving at a slower pace, motioning to a fallen trunk a little way off the path.

"One of the Lords of Chaos has got into our world," began Kate.

Morgan's face darkened as they told him what had happened at the Chapel. He waited for them to reach the end of their story before he spoke again.

"Only one of the Great Ones could have done this and only now. They are feeding off Erda's power. This must have been a place where the barriers between the Worlds are breaking down. What did this woman look like?"

They described all that they could remember of her.

"And you would recognize the Water Witch?"

"Yes. It wasn't her."

Morgan's expression became even more serious.

"What is it?" David asked.

"Morgan?" Tisian was watching his face.

"Your friend opened the gate between the Worlds to the Queen of Darkness. With her in your world, the gate stands open for all the others. It is only one step now for them to force a way through to the Wildwood and the Heart of the Earth. They will try to hunt Erda down and force her into unleashing all her power.

"We must find her and hide her from them, make her understand what is at stake; what we need her to do."

"I thought," said Kate cautiously, "that we were going to help her escape; to go back to wherever it is she comes from."

Morgan's expression hardened.

"There is no hope for the Worlds now that the Lords have broken through, unless Erda walks into the Heart of the Earth."

"What about the Guardians? Surely they can fight against the Lords of Chaos?" said David.

"Remember, they brought Erda here so that she would walk into the fire. They will not help her escape."

There was a heavy silence. Tisian fiddled with whatever held her hair in its untidy knot until it all slipped loose and fell about her shoulders.

"Where is she now?" she said to Morgan.

"In the Wildwood somewhere, but not close; and not human either."

"How do you know?" asked David.

"I can sense her. We are bound in some way. It has grown stronger ever since Thomas died."

"Is it the same for her? Can she tell where you are?" said Kate.

"I imagine so. I'm not sure."

"What should we do?" asked David.

"You must go back to your own world. Keep close to those you know well and be on your guard. Trust your instincts — you can recognize the Lords.

"If you are threatened, take refuge in the house. The Guardians strengthened it to stand against the Lords. I think it would survive even if the Lords triumph. You must not use the Door that brought you here again. If you do, the Lords may be able to follow you into the Wildwood and it will be lost. You should go now. I will come when I can."

The walk back to Tisian's house was a silent one. She hugged both the children before she lifted the patchwork aside.

"Good luck," said Morgan.

"You too," replied David. He lifted the latch and they stepped back into Mr Flowerdew's house.

17. The Hunt

The Queen of Darkness stood at the top of the little grassy meadow on which Kate and David had watched the rabbits hours before. Behind her the iron railing and the stone wall, which surrounded the Chapel, were indistinct in the gathering dusk.

She was satisfied with the afternoon's events, although it would have been even better if she could have tricked one of the children known to the Lightning King into inviting her to enter their world. The knowledge that they had done so would surely have destroyed them, in every way that mattered.

The King gathered himself from a swirl of dark air beside her and looked about him in silence, fascinated.

"Well?" said the Queen.

"Even better than I remembered. Of course, we have been forced here to do battle all the other times, not invited in." He smiled his wolf's smile.

The Queen, gowned tonight in the colour of a thundercloud and crowned with black sapphires strung on copper wire, smiled back at him.

"Where is Tethys?"

He hissed. "Still sulking. She is sure to be plotting something."

"If *he* finds out…"

"She knows what risks she runs."

The air stirred behind them and they turned to see the Hunter stepping through into the world. He sniffed the air deeply, nostrils flared, eyes closed. When he opened them he looked around, taking no heed of the growing dark, but looking past it to those things that caught his notice.

"The others?"

"They are gathering," said the King. "They wait for a signal."

"Not yet," said the Queen quickly.

"No," said the Hunter. "My worthless son has not yet found the Stardreamer." The others said nothing. "Tethys, I suppose, is planning vengeance?"

"Perhaps," agreed the King.

"Then it seems we have time to spare. Time for some sport."

He threw back his head and gave voice like a hound that follows a scent. The ground below them shuddered and out of the hillside poured the Wild Hunt.

No more than a half-remembered legend in this world, until this night, the creatures of the Hunt milled about the Hunter as he walked to its head between scything teeth and murderous claws. He looked back at the Queen of Darkness and the Lightning King.

"Do you ride with us tonight?"

"No," said the Queen. "There are plans to lay. We must be ready."

"I am ready now," said the Hunter with his dreadful smile, turning to go. He paused and looked back. "Tell Tethys that if she makes a move I will let the Hunt have her." With that, the Hunt leapt into the air and disappeared into the darkness, its cries trailing higher and higher into the sky.

The King raised an eyebrow as he looked at the Queen. "We cannot protect her, can we?"

"Would you wish to try?"

He shook his head.

Nightmares such as they had never known tore through the sleep of those whose homes lay below the Hunt's path. Children woke screaming and adults sobbing, from dreams of the wreck and loss of all that they loved. Lights burned through the night and families held each other for comfort from the inexplicable terror that gripped them.

They greeted the morning with relief, red-eyed and haunted and already dreading the night to come, although there was no reason: they were just dreams, that's all, not so frightful in daylight, everything was fine, hush now.

Deep in the Wildwood, Morgan called to Erda. Sitting, he put aside his bow and closed his eyes. He visualized the connection between them as a shining ribbon and poured his thought into it, making it broader and stronger, until it would carry his thoughts to her. He knew that she was attending to what he did and that, for the moment, she was not retreating from it. He tried to hold back the knowledge of what he wanted her to do, although he no longer knew if that was possible. Perhaps to her his thoughts were transparent as glass.

The message he poured into and along the ribbon was simple. *Come to me. Talk to me.* He repeated it over and over, heedless of the sun moving above him, of the waning of the day. When at last he stopped, too weary to continue, he was surprised to find it was nearly dusk and that Tisian was sitting by a little fire close by, swaddled in blankets.

When she saw him rouse himself she came to where he sat and offered him her hand. He took it gratefully, so stiff and cold that he could hardly get up. She threw a blanket round his shoulders and led him over to the fire and poured him a cup of hot heather beer.

"Do you think she will come?" she said.

He shrugged, hands wrapped round the cup to warm

them. "If she wants to. I know she hears me. Perhaps she knows every thought in my head. I can't tell any more." He yawned hugely.

"Come back to the house and sleep. I have a feeling there will be few peaceful nights left us before the end comes, whatever it brings."

He nodded and drank the rest of his beer.

Deep in the night, when there was no light but the glow from the hearth, Morgan woke suddenly from a dreamless sleep. From where he lay on a makeshift mattress near the fire, he could make out the humped shape of Tisian in the alcove bed, snoring gently. He pulled the blankets closer round his shoulders and turned over.

Erda sat cross legged on the table, the air around her glowing faintly. Morgan caught his breath and stopped moving.

"It's all right. I've been waiting for you to wake up," she said. He sat up slowly, glancing round to where Tisian lay. "She won't hear us," said Erda and Morgan had no doubt of it. "You never told me what you want from me," she continued.

He began to speak, to try somehow to explain, but she silenced him with a wave of her hand.

"Not yet. I came to tell you that I will listen to you, but not here and not yet. First I want to speak to Kate and David again. You can find me there. I will not hide from you any longer. I am tired of hiding."

Before he could say anything in reply she had gone and he was aware, for the first time, of how empty was the space where she had been.

In Kate and David's world it was already dawn. A small spider crept under the door and into Kate's bedroom, dim behind drawn curtains, and a moment later

Erda stood looking down at the sleeping girl. She moved to the window and twitched the curtains open a little. A bar of light fell across Kate's face and after a few seconds she stirred and opened her eyes.

At first she thought that the figure silhouetted against the window was her mother, then she realized with a start that it was Erda.

"Where have you been? How did you get in?"

Erda ignored the questions and came over to sit down on the bed as Kate pushed her sleep-draggled hair out of her eyes. They studied each other closely for a moment.

"What's happening to you?" asked Kate.

"What is meant to happen, I think. I do not know. Something — I do not know the word for it — grows inside me. Soon I will no longer be able to control it and it will break free. Morgan fears this and longs for it too. I do not understand yet, but soon I will. I see with his mind more clearly each day."

"Erda," said Kate more urgently, "you must go. Not just from here; you must go back to wherever you came from — to the stars if that's where it was. People here are trying to use you. They don't care about you, just about getting what they want. You can still escape, but I don't think you have much time."

"How would I escape?"

"I don't know. Don't you know how to get back?"

"Perhaps. I should go. Your brother is waking up. He will come to your room soon." She paused and looked hard at Kate again. "You still blame yourself. You must let go of that guilt or you will be too weak to help."

Kate had no idea what she meant. She took her eyes off Erda for a moment and found, when she looked back, that she had gone.

David had woken early. It was often the case in

summer, usually because he forgot to draw his curtains; but this morning he was just awake. He lay in
bed reading, watching the hands of his alarm clock
crawl round the face. There was a soft knock on the
door.

"Yeah?"

Naturally, he was expecting Dad or Christine when
the door opened, but instead it was Erda who came in.
She smiled at the look of surprise on his face. He put a
finger to his lips.

"Someone might hear you," he hissed.

She shook her head, her gaze wandering around his
posters and books and general organized mess.

"They won't."

"You have to get out of here quickly. The Lords of
Chaos are after you. They want to use you to break the
Worlds apart or something."

"What are the Lords of Chaos?" she asked puzzled,
then looked into his mind to find the words that would
tell her.

"Ah, those ones. I do not fear them. They cannot
hurt me."

"But they'll do something. They'll make you ... I
don't know. Morgan knows; he'll tell you. He's been
trying to find you."

"I know. I told him I would meet him in your world
and listen to him once I had spoken to you and Kate. I
went to her before I came here."

She picked up a shuttlecock, turned it in her fingers
for a moment, then put it down.

"I want you and Kate to be there when I meet him. I
will go back to the house and call him and wait. When
can you be there?"

"Umm ..." He looked at his clock. Six fifteen. "Hang
on, I'll try to phone Kate." He got out of bed and scrab-

bled for his phone. After a moment, Kate answered, wide awake. David didn't waste time.

"Erda's here. She wants us all to meet at the house. Can you be there by eight?"

There was a pause before Kate said "Okay. I'll say I'm coming over to your place and meet you there. But David, I'm not promising anything."

"What do you mean?"

"You know I don't want this any more."

There was no sense trying to argue with her on the phone.

"See you then."

Erda had gone by the time he put the phone down.

Morgan had followed Erda as best he could as soon as he realized where she had gone. He wondered if he should wait in the house, but time lay too heavy there. When he left its protection he could feel it at once, like a trace of some scent on the air. The Lords were here.

Restlessness kept him moving until he found himself on the edge of a park at the foot of a steep hill, bounded by a gated iron fence. Beyond the fence was a small house with a red-tiled roof, and a green wooden sign that read "Blackford Pond. Local Nature Reserve." Even before he went in he could hear the sound of ducks and coots.

A path took him to the pond on which the birds sailed, carefree in the morning light. Though it was a popular spot, with benches all around the pond, at this time of morning it was deserted. He walked slowly round the edge, glad to be away from roads and buildings.

About halfway round, he realized he was not alone. There was a little island in the middle of the pond, barely a foot above the water. On it sat a woman, her face in her hands, sobbing. She must have fallen in somehow, for her long brown hair and dress were soaking wet, water streaming off them and disappearing into the earth around her.

"What's wrong? Do you need help?" Morgan called, but she continued to sob. She seemed quite unaware of his presence.

The water was clear enough for him to see the bottom of the pond and so shallow it would hardly reach his knees. He stepped in and began to walk across to the island.

He was halfway there when the birds went silent. He stopped and looked at where they floated, voiceless. When he turned back to the island the woman was standing, watching him, no longer sobbing, though the water poured ceaselessly from her hair and clothes. She stretched her crimson mouth in a smile and raised her arms.

The world exploded around Morgan just as he realized who it was on the island. The waters of the pond gathered themselves to Tethys' hands and hurtled at him and the bottom of the pond disappeared from under his feet.

He was submerged, tumbling over and over under the onslaught of the water. He tried to kick for the surface, but he didn't even know in which direction it was.

He thought of Erda and Tisian and the Wildwood, and of Thomas, and of how he had failed them all. His breath was running out. He kicked desperately for the surface again, but it wasn't there.

If only ...

If only ...

18. Consequences

Morgan drifted in the dark, at peace at last, ready for death. Any second now he would take a breath and his lungs would fill with water and there would be an end of everything …

Someone grabbed his shoulder; a terrible grip that seemed to grind its way into his bones. Whoever it was dragged his head out of the water just as he took his final breath, so that it was part water, but mostly air, and hurled him onto the bank.

As he lay coughing and retching he could hear voices. One, Tethys presumably, shouted, "He killed my wolves; I will have vengeance. Do not interfere."

The other voice was much quieter, but its sound made Morgan's skin crawl.

"I warned you not to touch him. I told you what would happen." There was a sound like the cry of a hunting dog and after a second, answering cries and yelps, like the belling of a pack of hounds. Tethys shrieked, "No!" and Morgan lifted his head and saw, through his soaked lashes, Tethys and the other figure, the one from his nightmares, struggling in the water. Beyond them he could dimly make out shapes, swift and terrible, rushing towards them.

Tethys gave another scream and the pond became a whirlpool. The water boiled around them briefly, then they were gone.

Morgan let his head drop and lay, gasping for breath. When he was able to sit up he looked at the pond again. It lay tranquil under the morning sun, a swan sailing past the island with unruffled grace.

"What happened?" From somewhere, Erda

appeared at his side. When he tried to speak he started coughing, so she took it from his mind instead. She sat down with a thump on the bank beside him, her face stricken.

"What is it?" he managed to ask.

"This is my doing."

"What?"

"The wolves. You killed them to try and keep me safe — and I let you. There was no need; they could not have harmed me. But now, all this because of that … One thing makes so many others happen here. How does anyone dare to do anything at all?"

"Consequences."

"What?"

"The things that happen because of something else. They're called consequences."

She nodded absently. "We must go back to the house now. Kate and David will come soon." She stood and held out a hand to him and pulled him, with surprising ease, to his feet.

In the Underworld, close to Lake Avernus, the Hunt caught up with Tethys and made an end of her as the Hunter watched, smiling.

"Maybe they're not coming," said Kate, looking out the window again.

"It's only just gone eight. They'll be here. Why don't you sit down?" David tried to sound soothing, but Kate's nervy pacing was unsettling him too.

"I don't want to be here. If they don't come by ten past, I'm going."

David bit back the urge to yell at her. He couldn't understand why she was being like this. She must realize as he did, deep down, that once again there was no walking away from this. He decided it was probably best to say nothing.

Kate's pacing took her back to the window yet again.

"They're here. What on earth ...?" She made for the front door without completing the sentence.

Erda looked upset and Morgan was soaked through, though it wasn't raining, hadn't rained in days.

"What happened to you?" asked David. Morgan shook his head.

"Not now. It doesn't matter." They obviously didn't believe that, but accepted it for the moment, to his relief. He found what had just happened frightening enough; he didn't want to pass that fear on to Kate or David.

They found him some dry clothes and went to hang his wet stuff in the garden. As he dressed, he noticed that his shoulder was already a mass of purple bruises where he'd been dragged out of the water, and when he caught sight of his face in a mirror he was shocked by how awful he looked; white-faced and grim. He tried smiling, but it looked even worse. Rubbing his aching shoulder, he went to join the others in the kitchen.

It was Erda who had brought them together, so now they waited for her to speak.

"Who brought me here?" she asked, looking from face to face. "Someone called and brought me to the Worlds. Was it one of you?"

"None of us has the power to do that. Only the Guardians of Time or the Lords of Chaos could do that. The Guardians called you down."

"I have heard you speak of the Lords of Chaos, but who are these Guardians?" They started to explain and soon she had taken enough words from their heads to understand. "I sense them, but they do not know I am here. None are close."

It took a few seconds for the import of her words to sink in.

"But they must know you're here if they brought you," reasoned Kate.

"Then it cannot be them who called me. It must have been the others."

Morgan stood up so abruptly that his chair tipped over with a clatter onto the tiles. He walked out of the back door without a word and they stared, baffled, as he stumbled to the other end of the garden like a blind man and finished leaning against a tree.

"What's wrong with him?" Kate said

"I don't know. It's something to do with what Erda just said. Should I go out there?"

Erda laid a hand on his arm and shook her head. "You must leave him. He thought he knew who he was. Now he doubts it." Her words made no sense at all.

In the garden, Morgan struggled with the horror that threatened to overcome him …

The Guardians had summoned him to search for the Stardreamer. It *must have* been the Guardians. He hadn't seen them of course … he *never* saw anyone in the Empty Place; they were just presences, without form, but it *must* have been the Guardians.

You assumed it was them who called you; who used you. You would never let the idea that it might be the Lords into your head, would you?

What had he done?

"Are you saying it was the Lords of Chaos who brought you here?" asked David, sure he must have got something wrong.

"I don't know. It could not have been these Guardians; even now they do not know I am here.

Morgan says the Lords are the only other ones who could have done it."

"Does that mean you're really on their side?" It was the question Kate had dreaded asking.

Erda frowned. "I am myself. I am not on anyone's side."

In the garden, Morgan stood with his eyes shut, trying to remember ...

His mother had told him of his kinship to the Lords and the Guardians, but it was always his inheritance from the Guardians that she spoke of as shaping him ... *She would say that, wouldn't she? She was your mother; she loved you, she wanted to protect you.*

The times he'd been called to the Empty Place and set some task or other by the Guardians he'd never seen anyone of course. He'd just assumed it must be the Guardians, but looking back with the cold eyes of hopelessness, it seemed to him that it could as easily have been the Lords who had sent him on these errands, toying with him for their own amusement.

He sent his mind back to the summons that had set him on this path ...

The cold mist of the Empty Place had swirled about him. There had been voices around him, but he could never see the source.

"The Stardreamer must be found and brought to the Heart of the Earth."

"If the power of the Stardreamer is joined with the Heart of the Earth then the Worlds will be safe. The Dream will hold them safe; but if the power of the Stardreamer is loosed outside, it will destroy the Heart of the Earth and the walls between the Worlds and the Lords of Chaos will triumph utterly."

He had wanted to believe that the Guardians had

summoned him to help save the Worlds. Now it seemed that the Lords had brought him there to trick him into helping destroy them.

"What are you going to do?" It was David who broke the silence that had fallen in the kitchen. Erda didn't answer. She was watching Morgan make his way back up the garden, shoulders bowed as though he carried a great weight. When he came in he looked at their expectant faces, then spoke.

"You must go Erda. I've betrayed you. All this time I thought I was searching for you for the Guardians; that it was them who had called you and whose bidding I was doing. I have been tricked. The Lords have directed everything I've done. I didn't know until I heard what you said just now.

"I've failed you all, betrayed you all. All my life I thought I was working for the Light and now I find that the Darkness has claimed me."

Erda's expression was unreadable. 'Would it not have been a betrayal then, if the Guardians had sent you? You searched for me to make me join with the Heart of the Earth. Whichever side sent you only wanted to use me for its own ends.'

"You're right," said Morgan. "Of course you're right. It was *all* a betrayal. You should go now. You must know enough about your power to be able to return to the stars if that is what you want."

She nodded in agreement. "From this place I could go. I can see the path now where I fell. I could follow it back."

"I will not stand in your way."

"But what about the Worlds, the Lords?" gasped David.

"They're not her responsibility," said Morgan,

"they're ours. Those of us who live here will have to find a way to save the Worlds, to force the Lords back into the Underworld. The Guardians will help."

"What will you do, Kate?" Erda said unexpectedly.

"I don't want to have to do anything," said Kate slowly. "I want everything to be normal again."

"I know. I'm sorry." Erda looked from face to face as though trying to fix them in her mind. "I must go now. The Hunt is gathering. The Lords know I am here. Soon they will come. Do not let them find the Door to the Wildwood. Keep the house safe."

"Will we see you again?" David could hardly get the words out.

"I do not think so. I want to see everything."

A breeze swirled up from the floor and stroked their faces as it passed and Erda became part of it.

Morgan sat down at the big kitchen table, staring into nothing. In Kate's mind an urgent curiosity fought with an unwillingness to intrude. Curiosity won.

"You said something about Light and Darkness just now. What did you mean?"

He looked up, surprised. "Surely you know? It is the heritage of the Guardians and the Lords, that you carry too. I am a Child of Light and Darkness, like you." He saw the look of shock on her face. "You didn't know?"

"We only just found out about ourselves," replied David. "We found a letter from Mr Flowerdew — the Guardian — a few days ago that told us."

"But this is … only those like us can pass through the Doors or have the strength to fight for one side against the other. Did he not tell you when you fought with the Guardians before?"

Kate shook her head. "No. I think he was trying to protect us from knowing about the Darkness inside us.

Have you known all your life?"

"Almost. My mother told me when I was ten." He told them the tale of the Traveller at the Ford.

Wide-eyed, Kate asked, "How have you coped, knowing that about yourself?"

He shrugged. "By not letting it shape me. We all inherit something from our parents, but in the end, we make ourselves. The Darkness need not control us, any more than the Light. Think of your parents; at least one of them must be like you in this, maybe both. Your small brother too, Kate." He gave a thin smile. "There are more of us than you think."

Kate was deep in thought, but David fidgeted, anxious to ask a quite different question.

"Has Erda gone back to the stars. Can you tell?"

"She has not gone yet. She is far away in this world, moving fast. She said she wanted to see everything. I think she will come back once she has looked at your world again."

A melancholy descended on them and they sat in silence for a while before Morgan roused himself and went to get his clothes, already almost dry in the morning sun. David looked at his watch.

"It's half past nine. School will be trying to get hold of our parents to find out why we're not there."

"They'll be livid."

"Or worried."

Morgan came back in, looking more troubled than ever.

"Can you feel it? The Lords are gathering. The house will not be easy for them to find, but they are drawing closer. They follow the trail of Erda's power. We must be ready for them: the house must stay safe until Erda has escaped. After that ... I do not know what will happen to us."

"How can we stop them getting into the house?" asked David.

"I don't think they can break down doors or force their way in in any way unless Erda releases all her power. At first they will try to persuade or frighten or trick their way in. We must refuse, whatever form they take. The inside of this house is the safest place there will be once the battle begins, but I do not know what will happen to the world outside when the Hunt comes. For those nearby it will be terrible."

David checked his watch again. Dad and Christine would be at work by now, away on the other side of town, Kate's mum too, and her Dad was working on a job in Longniddry, down the coast.

"At least our families ..." he began, and than saw Kate's stricken face.

"Ben..."

19. Dust Devils

Ben's school wasn't even four hundred yards from the house. He certainly wasn't safe.

"I have to go and get him," said Kate.

"What?" said Morgan, disturbed from some thought of his own.

"My little brother. He's in school, just along the road. He's too close to be safe if things go badly. I've got to go and get him and bring him to the house. He'll be safer here, won't he?"

"Perhaps." He still seemed distracted. "If you mean to go, you must do so quickly. Soon it will be impossible to leave."

She nodded and took a deep breath. "I'll go now. Will you come with me David?"

"No." Morgan cut off David's reply. "Someone must stay here."

"But you'll be here," said David.

"I have to leave."

"What?"

"You can't leave us."

"I must. I think Erda has misled us. She doesn't mean to come back here — remember, she said she didn't think she'd see you again."

"Then where ...?"

"I think she is going to the Heart of the Earth. I have to go there to try and stop whatever is about to happen."

"Can't you wait until I come back?"

"No. I must go now and you should do the same."

David fought down a rising sense of panic. "I can't do this on my own."

"You won't have to. There is still a little time: time for Kate to do this.

"If Erda has gone to the Heart of the Earth it is even more important that the Lords do not enter this house. If they get in they will pour through the Door to the Wildwood. You must hold them back." He started up the stairs. "Believe in yourselves. You have already shown you have the strength to do this." He paused and looked back at them. "I will do my best to bring Erda back and to come back myself. Good luck."

David went with Kate to the front door. They opened it a little and looked out, not knowing what to expect.

Though the street was deserted, everything seemed more or less normal except for the light. A reddish-brown haze seemed to hang in the air, like mist or smoke. Kate looked at David's pinched face.

"I have to try and save Ben. If something happened to him that I could have stopped I'd never be able to forgive myself."

He nodded. "Don't be long."

She set off at a run.

As soon as she left the protection of the front garden, she realized that things were far from normal. The air seemed thick and heavy and left a metallic taste in her mouth when she breathed it in. There was no one else out in the street at all, so far as she could see. She jogged along as best she could, trying to keep fear at bay.

She found that the oppressive feeling around her lessened as she moved away from the house. When she looked back it was a blurred image in the rusty air, the centre of the disturbance. She turned her mind to how she was going to get Ben out of school. What if the teacher wouldn't let her take him? She'd just have to find a way somehow. This time she wouldn't let him down.

In the house, David watched Kate's receding figure. He felt very alone and completely at a loss as to what to do. For something to occupy a few minutes he went round the house locking all the windows and closing and fastening the shutters, except in the bedroom above the front door from where he would watch for Kate's return. He didn't imagine that window locks were likely to be any sort of defence against what was going to be trying to get in, but it was less unbearable than waiting, doing nothing.

When he'd finished he went to his watching place. In the rusty air outside, little spirals of dust were beginning to coalesce here and there.

By the time Kate reached the school, the air looked almost normal and the weight that seemed to press on her had lessened. She paused for a second at the door and looked back, but there was no sign of anyone or anything following her. She pressed the buzzer and waited to be let in.

"Yes?" the secretary's voice, distorted by the intercom.

"It's Ben Dalgliesh's sister with a message for him."

"All right."

She heard the lock click and pushed the door open and forced herself to smile at the faces in the office as she went past. As she took the stairs two at a time she cursed the fact that Ben's classroom was at the very top of the building, just under the eaves.

At the top she stopped to catch her breath before she knocked on the door. *Oh well, here goes.* She didn't have much of a plan but she wasn't going to come up with anything better in the next few minutes.

"Come in."

She pushed the door open and went in smiling.

"Sorry to disturb you. Could I have a quick word with Ben please? There's a change of plan for who's picking him up this afternoon."

"Yes, of course, but shouldn't you be in school, Kate?" Trust her old teacher, Mrs Henderson, to ask.

"Mum's taking me to the dentist. She's outside in the car. She couldn't find a parking space, so she sent me up."

Mrs Henderson made a sympathetic noise. "The parking's ridiculous around here. I hardly ever get a space near the school. Go on then, no problem."

"Thanks. I'll just explain outside the door so I don't disturb your class *too* much."

Ben looked baffled. Kate smiled brightly at him. "Come outside for a minute, Ben, so I can talk to you." As soon as the door shut behind them she grabbed his hand and pulled him towards the stairs. "Come on Ben. You have to come with me. It's really important."

"What? You said you wanted to talk to me."

She started down the stairs, still gripping his hand so that he had no alternative but to follow her.

"Stop it, Kate." His voice was rising. "Where are we going?"

She paused for a moment. "It's a surprise. To make up for the car hitting you. I'm taking you on a special adventure."

His eyes widened. "Cool," he breathed. "What is it?"

"It's a secret. You'll see soon, but we have to hurry." She started down the stairs again and this time he kept up with her willingly. "Ben, keep quiet while we go past the office. Let's see if we can get past without them noticing. Like spies."

He nodded, ripe for adventure now.

Expecting every second to hear Mrs Henderson's voice high above them, Kate pushed Ben past the open office door and tiptoed after him, then eased the front door open as quietly as possible.

They were out. She heaved a sigh of relief. So far, so good.

"Kate, why is everything that funny colour?"

She turned from the door, a cold knot in the pit of her stomach. The air was full of reddish particles, like clay dust or very fine sand. She tried to keep her voice light as she said, "Isn't that strange? Maybe it's a sandstorm. Come on, we need to go quickly."

"Don't be stupid. You don't get sandstorms here. Where are we going anyway?"

She grabbed his hand again and pulled him along at a half run. "Wait and see. It's not far."

The dust was forming spirals, like tiny whirlwinds.

"Wow, look at that!"

The little dust spirals were merging, growing larger as they did so.

"Come on, Ben, go a bit faster."

He picked up the note of worry in her voice. "What's wrong?"

"Nothing. We just don't want to be late, that's all."

There was a single dust spiral now, tall as a man and moving in parallel with them on the other side of the road. Kate felt fear begin to beat in her blood. The thickening air seemed to slow their movements and to press on her chest so that it was difficult to breathe. She forced her way on, Ben trailing at her side, eyes fixed on the whirling dust.

They were only a couple of hundred metres from the house now, but it seemed very far away in the murky light. She thought she could make out David's figure at one of the windows. At her side, Ben gasped and gripped her hand hard.

"Kate, what's that? What's happening? I don't like it. Make it go away."

As he spoke, the whirlwind of dust overtook them and from it, something began to emerge, as though shaping itself out of the dust.

It most closely resembled a dog, though it wasn't one. Larger than a Great Dane, with a rough pelt the colour of the dust from which it was making itself, it eased free of the whirlwind limb by limb. Its eyes were like green lamps, its lolling tongue was scarlet and its yellow teeth were like knives. Spittle trailed from its mouth in long, blood-flecked strings.

Ben whimpered and pressed himself close to Kate's side, robbed of speech by fear, but somehow Kate's brain had passed beyond fear and into some kind of survival state she hadn't known she possessed.

The beast was not yet fully formed, one leg and much of its hindquarters still swirling in a cloud of dust. Once it got free it would be between them and the house and they would have no chance. They had to act now.

"Run!" she yelled to Ben and hauled him off at a sprint past the terrible slavering jaws. As she did so a gleam of light appeared through the gloom as David opened the front door.

A hundred and fifty metres, all down hill. Could they do it? How long until the beast got free?

A hundred metres; behind Kate and Ben a dreadful howling.

"Come on, Ben, there's David. We can do it," she gasped.

She glanced back over her shoulder and realized they couldn't. The thing was bounding down the hill after them, catching up with every stride. She let go of Ben's hand.

"Keep going; I'll catch up," she shouted and stopped running. She turned to face the beast. Thirty metres from her it slowed to a trot, unused to having any quarry turn to face it.

So terrified she could hardly breathe, she glanced around for anything she could use as a weapon. Nothing. Not a stick or a stone. She began to back away slowly. The beast paused, a low rumbling growl rising in its throat. In the gutter lay an old broom handle that someone had put out with the rubbish. Her eyes never leaving the beast, she bent and picked it up with shaking fingers and kept backing.

She saw the hound gather itself to spring, fangs bared, and fighting down a suicidal impulse to turn and run, gripped the broom handle as tight as she could.

The beast sprang. Kate screamed and lashed out blindly with her pitiful weapon. She felt it connect and then break and the creature was on the ground, snarling, one ear torn open. Broken in half, the broom handle was now virtually useless.

Kate realized it would all be over in a few seconds. There was no point running and she couldn't fight this thing, not alone. Why did nobody come out from the houses to help?

"Help!" she shouted at the top of her voice. "Somebody help me!" At that moment a swirl of icy wind wound around her like a cocoon and she felt *something* within her snap and break free.

The wind whipped away again and she stood alone, facing the beast, but now it was different. She felt something like electricity flooding through her, filling her up to her fingertips. "Go away!" she shouted. "Leave us alone!"

The hound swung its head this way and that, scenting, puzzled. It growled again but did not spring and made no attempt now to come after her as she moved away slowly, still facing it.

She noticed other dust clouds whirling and shapes beginning to gather themselves inside. Trying to ignore them, she kept moving, Ben and David's shouts urging her on until there was the gate and the open door and then she did turn and run, and together they slammed the door shut and collapsed in a heap on the hall floor.

20. Siege

"I will do my best to bring Erda back and to come back myself. Good luck," Morgan had said, looking down at the children's appalled faces from halfway up the stairs. He turned away from them before he lost his resolve and hurried to the little bedroom where the Door to the Wildwood was hidden.

Agitated as he was, it took him several attempts before the Door opened into Tisian's house. He pushed aside the patchwork and immediately felt Erda's presence somewhere far off in the wood.

Tisian sat smoking in front of the fire, eyes fixed on him. It looked as though she had been waiting for him.

"She was here," she said without preamble. "Showed herself to me properly, sat and talked for a bit. Poor lass. We've trapped her properly between the lot of us."

"No we haven't. I'm trying to catch up with her to persuade her to go back to the stars." He dropped into the chair opposite her. "It was Kate that made me see properly what I was doing, trying to trap her. I don't want her to go into the Heart of the Earth. I want her to escape and then those of us that can will have to try and put this mess right ourselves."

Tisian looked at him, but didn't speak.

"What? Why are you looking at me like that?"

"It seems to me Erda understands things a lot better than you do, lad."

He didn't understand, but there was no time to sit here debating. "Did she say where she was heading?"

"Don't interfere Morgan. Let her be." Something — was it fear? — moved in Tisian's eyes.

"She's going to the Heart of the Earth. She told you, didn't she?"

"Don't go after her. What can you do, if she's decided? How can you stop her?"

"I don't know, but I have to try. Did she tell you it was the Lords who brought her, not the Guardians? They're besieging the house on the other side of your Door because they think she's there. If she goes to the Heart of the Earth they will do something to make her release her power outside it. Even if I wanted her to walk into the fire the risk is too great."

Tisian's face had grown pale. "No, she didn't tell me, but it makes no difference. They would have tried to do the same if the Guardians had called her."

"But the Guardians would have been with her to keep her safe."

"Maybe no one can keep her safe but herself."

Morgan pushed himself out of the chair. "I have to go. If there is anything you can do to strengthen the Door from this side, do it. We must keep the Lords out for as long as possible." He pulled Tisian to her feet and gave her a quick, hard hug. "I'll come back and I'll bring her with me if I can."

He ducked out of the door and set off at a trot towards the Heart of the Earth. From the doorway, Tisian watched him out of sight.

Standing on the wind in the treetops far away in the Wildwood, Erda listened to what Tisian and Morgan said. She would have liked to spend more time with Tisian, but it seemed that time was one thing she did not have.

She kept part of her mind trained on Kate and David. David was alone in the house and Kate had gone to the school. The Hunt was drawing close.

The ones she recognized as the leaders were somewhere else entirely though, trying to blast their way through the barriers around this world using some of the power that, despite her efforts to contain it, now bled from her continuously. She could not wait much longer.

She took a last, yearning look at the Wildwood and all its living things and prepared to travel for the final time. She heard Kate's voice in her head. *Help! Somebody help me!*

One of the Hunter's creatures, with a coat the colour of clay and huge yellow fangs, was ready to spring at her as she tried to keep it at bay while her small brother ran pell-mell for the house.

Erda needed no time to think. She stretched out to where Kate was and enveloped her and allowed as much power as was safe to flow into her. Enough at least to defeat this thing, she thought, but there was no time to do more. The Lords were coming.

She withdrew and sent herself along the arrow of her own thoughts to the Heart of the Earth.

David turned every lock on the front door as Kate and Ben picked themselves off the floor. Ben was crying noisily.

"I want to go back to school. That dog tried to eat me!"

Although she was absolutely white, Kate sounded quite calm. "Well, you can't go out with that horrible stray dog around, can you? We'll have to wait for someone to catch it. There's lots of chocolate and biscuits in the kitchen. Do you want some while we wait?"

Ben's cries subsided to a snuffle. "Yes. Chocolate. Where is it?"

Face to face with David over Ben's head, Kate rolled her eyes and managed a smile. "Come on, I'll show you."

They disappeared into the kitchen and after a short pause, Kate emerged alone.

"We're just going upstairs for a minute," she called to Ben and they went up to the room from which David had been keeping watch.

From the window they looked down through the gritty air to the shapes that were emerging from the vortices of dust.

"What are they?" breathed Kate.

"Chaos creatures, I suppose ..."

Out of the dust came creatures that were almost like hounds, and great hunting cats striped like silk, and things that flew, but were not birds.

There were ten altogether, including the one that Kate had already faced, dark blood still dripping from its torn ear. So far they flew and prowled aimlessly, not yet focused on the house or its occupants.

"Do you think this is all?"

"I hope so, but I doubt it, don't you? There's no way they could get inside. The shutters would keep them out."

"I'd better go down and see how Ben is."

They closed the shutters in this room too before they went out.

"Kate — something happened to you back there — when you hit the dog-thing. You're ... different. What happened?"

She paused, halfway down the stairs.

"I don't know exactly. It was like`... you know if you trip and nearly fall but you don't? There's that sort of whoosh goes through you; a prickling, like electricity." David nodded. "It was like that, but more so; and it's still there." She held her hands out in front of her face. "Like a tingling in my fingers."

"Some sort of power," said David. "It must be. It

made that thing stop and think anyway. Power from inside you; from the Light."

Kate was silent as she reached the bottom of the stairs.

"Kate?"

She turned back to him.

"It must be from the Light: it helped you save Ben, didn't it?"

She smiled. "Yes. Yes it did."

Ben had forgotten his fears and was munching his way through a bar of chocolate. "What's the adventure going to be?"

"Well ..." Kate thought fast, "We have to guard the house from some of our friends who're pretending to be baddies."

Ben curled his lip. "That's not an adventure. That's just stupid."

"Wait and see," said David. "They've got to try to scare us into giving up and letting them in," he went on, inventing madly, "and they've got one of these new virtual reality projectors — you must have seen the adverts on TV?" Ben nodded, open-mouthed. "They're making up really scary things with it and trying to convince us they're real."

"Wow! When do they start?"

"They already did," chimed in Kate, warming to the theme. "All that stuff on the way back from school — that was them."

Ben narrowed his eyes suspiciously. "Why were you frightened then, if it wasn't real?"

"I was pretending, so they'd think it was going to be easy," she replied triumphantly. "Come on, let's go upstairs and have a look."

As Ben eagerly led the way, Kate whispered to David, "How did you come up with that?"

David gave a quick grin. "Dad's always telling me I read too much science fiction. I knew it would come in useful sometime."

They opened the shutters a little and peered out. It was dim as twilight outside and in the murk they could see that there were more beasts than there had been before. There seemed to be six flying and at least a dozen on the ground, still moving in a disordered way, but all close to the house, though so far they seemed unwilling, or unable, to cross the boundary of the garden.

"We should check the back," said David.

"Those are good," said Ben approvingly. "They almost look real."

They went up to Mr Flowerdew's study and cautiously unshuttered the window. Apart from the colour of the air there seemed nothing out of the ordinary at the moment.

"Now what?" asked Kate.

"We wait, I suppose. Let's go back to the front and keep watch."

The Heart of the Earth burned with a steady, green-white fire, making no sound, consuming no fuel. Erda stared at it, the flames reflected from her eyes and from the glittering crystals in the walls of the cave. Constantly now, she had to fight to contain the power building up inside her. Soon it would become impossible; even now it bled constantly from her a little at a time, and she knew that the Lords fed on it. She could feel them trying to force a way through; soon they would have enough strength. She heard Morgan call her name and stepped out of the cave into the sunlight.

He had run more or less all the way and was breathing hard as he called her, unsure whether he was in

time to stop her. His relief when she stepped out of the
cave almost brought him to his knees.

"I thought I was too late," he gasped. "Don't do it
Erda. Come back to the house with me and you can
still escape."

"I cannot."

"Yes you can." He paused to catch his breath. "When
I found you I wanted to trap you into accepting this
fate. I wanted you to merge with the Heart of the
Earth and become the soul of these Worlds. I didn't
know ... I didn't even think about you. I thought it was
enough that I loved the Wildwood and the other
Worlds. I wanted so much to save them; but even to do
that, this price is too high."

In the background, at the edge of hearing, was a
grinding noise, the sound of the Lords breaking down
the barriers between the Worlds.

"I don't want to trap you into doing this. There is
still time. Go now and you can be free of all of us."

A blast of cold air hit them like a shout and now, on
the chill air, there were harsh voices.

"Go!" he shouted over the rising storm of noise.

21. The Stardreamer

In the short time that David, Kate and Ben had been in the study, things had changed. The beasts still prowled below, but now they pressed against the iron fence at the edge of the garden, their eyes constantly on the house. Beyond them, other figures began to shape themselves and step from the air.

It was hard to say what exactly they were, for they flickered, like images on a film being run at the wrong speed. Some were more or less human, but others were like the jumbled remains of animals and plants, trees and rocks and fog ... nightmare figures held together by willpower alone.

Kate choked back a sound in her throat as she saw Ben stare, wide-eyed, at the emerging horrors below.

"Now those are *good*," he said approvingly as Kate and David stared at him, astonished. Evidently they'd been more convincing than they'd thought.

"We should check the back again," said Kate.

They closed and locked the shutters and went back to the study. This time, as they unshuttered the window, something swooped past only a few feet away and they jumped back with a mutual gasp. Ben gave a nervous laugh.

David peered cautiously round the edge of the shutter. "There's three of them sitting on the garden wall."

Kate looked and as she did the three flying creatures spread leathery wings one after the other and crawled up the air towards them. They slammed the shutters closed again.

As Kate looked at David's pale, sweaty face — much like her own, she supposed — they heard a noise from

above them, from the roof; the sound of something
heavy struggling to find a foothold on the steeply slop-
ing slates, claws skidding.

They stared upwards, mesmerized. There was a
pause, then a loud snapping sound, then another.

"What's that?" Kate whispered.

"It sounds as though they're breaking the slates,"
said David, his gaze fixed on the ceiling. "That would
let them into the house."

"How can we stop them?"

"I've got no idea."

In unspoken agreement, they retreated down the
stairs to the hall. As they got to the foot of the steps, a
terrible noise started up outside, all the beasts howling
and crying out and behind it a wailing and grinding
from the other figures.

In the hall, the grandfather clock chimed once and
began to tick.

"Go while you can," Morgan had shouted over the tor-
rent of sound. Erda shaped herself into a handful of
dust and was gone in a swirl of air. Alone, Morgan
turned to face the wrath of the Lords of Chaos.

They stepped through the splintering air: Queen of
Darkness, Lightning King and Hunter. It seemed to
Morgan that all the noise drained out of the world as
they watched him.

It was the Queen who finally broke the insupport-
able silence. She took a step towards him, gowned in
the immeasurably dense blue of a winter dusk, diamonds wound around her throat and in her hair.

"So Morgan, we see what you truly are. A traitor,
forsworn — doubly forsworn, for you have served neither us nor the Stardreamer. I only wonder that she
has not struck you down herself." The Queen looked

about her. "Where is she? She has not gone into the fire. Where have you hidden her?"

"She is gone. Safe from all of you — all of us; from the Lords and the Guardians and from me."

"You let her go?"

"Yes."

The Queen laughed; an awful sound. "So you have found a third way to be forsworn; the Stardreamer, the Lords and now the Worlds as well. You are remarkable, Morgan."

Morgan kept silent, for he could feel that Erda was still close by.

"But she has not yet gone, has she Morgan?" the Lightning King asked. "You feel her presence, as we do."

Morgan said nothing. There was nothing he could deny. He was just what the Queen had said; forsworn. He had tried to betray Erda and had finished by betraying all the Worlds.

He knew that death awaited him here, on this little patch of dry grass. He would not try to evade it. How could he? All that remained to do, all that could redeem the smallest part of what he had done to everything he loved, was to give Erda a little more time to escape. He understood that it could not be long.

The sun was up and the air was full of birdsong. After all, this would not be too bad a place to make an end of things.

He brought his bow round from his back, slowly and deliberately, nocked an arrow and aimed at the place where the Queen's heart should be. She smiled and he let the arrow fly.

A bolt of lightning like a spear snapped the arrow in mid-flight and shattered his bow into a dozen pieces, throwing him off his feet and slamming him back against the rock wall at the mouth of the cave.

The Lightning King smiled a wolf-smile of pleasure at his shot.

Morgan shook his head to try and clear it as he sat up, wiping blood from his face where one of the shards of his bow had laid his cheek open. He looked into the beautiful, deadly face of the Queen of Darkness and watched her pluck a jewelled pin from her hair and breathe on it. It rose from her hand like some elegant insect and flew towards him.

"How could you be so foolish as to think that you could stand against us? See that you die well at least."

They stared at the grandfather clock for a moment, until a new sound took their attention.

"Ben? Ben I know you're in there. What's going on? Let me in."

"Mum?" Ben ran for the door. David grabbed him and held him, squirming. Kate looked out of the spy hole in the front door. Outside the door stood her mother. Most of the Chaos beasts were clustered beyond the fence, but two or three had braved the garden boundary and were picking their way towards the house.

Her mother was outside, in danger, calling Ben.

"Quick, Kate, let her in," Ben wailed.

Kate backed away from the door a little.

"No Ben, she's part of the pretend too. Think about it — Mum doesn't know you're here. How could she?"

David's father's voice was next, angry and imploring by turns. David stood beside the grandfather clock as though its ticking could drown out the rest of the sound, shaking his head.

Kate risked another look through the spy hole. The thing that wore her mother's face stared back, looking straight at her, while behind her and around her the beasts tore at the garden and began to push blindly at the walls of the house itself.

Suddenly her mother took a swift step forward, so that all Kate could see was an eye staring back at her from the other side of the door. Kate shot backwards and crashed into David, knocking him to the floor.

Ben stared at them. "Why are you both so scared if you know this is just a game?" From upstairs came the sound of breaking slates. "It is just a game, isn't it? Kate?"

But Kate wasn't listening any more. She was staring at the door as the letterbox was pushed open very slowly. A hand slid through, slowly, fingers feeling the way, and turned and moved towards the locks, the arm that supported it bending in such an un-natural way that Kate thought she was going to be sick.

Beside her, David scrambled to his feet then stood rooted with horror as the crawling hand found and turned the first lock.

Morgan got to his feet as the jewelled dart flew towards him. He pulled out his knife and tried to cut it down before it reached him, but it was much too fast, dodging the blade as though it was a living thing and striking him in the left side of his chest, the force spinning him round as he fell to his knees.

The dart burned like fire in his flesh, but even as he reached to pull it out, it melted away as though it had been made of ice. The wound though, was all too real, blood welling from it frighteningly fast. There would not be much more time for him.

The Hunter raised his terrible head, scenting blood.

Hanging as a drop of dew on the tip of a beech leaf high above, Erda watched the confrontation between Morgan and the Lords of Chaos.

It was growing more difficult to prevent the power bursting free. Below her she could sense it pulsing in the Lords of Chaos, could feel the assault on the house in Kate and David's world increasing in ferocity.

Betrayed. Forsworn.

The words drifted up to her and crawled into her head. She already knew what Morgan had intended when he first met her. He had been prepared to use her to save the Worlds because he loved them. He *loved* them; and yet he had drawn back and told her what he had planned, so that she would leave and be safe, because he loved her too.

And with that thought, she saw everything and understood everything and all the words in her head made sense at last and power blossomed within her like a flame.

She was aware of everything in all the Worlds in one incredible shock of knowledge: the stones, the leaves, the black deer in the Wildwood, Tisian staring into her fire, Kate and David in the house at the still centre of a storm of noise; and above all, Morgan. She looked down on the scene below and saw the Lightning King's spear fly and knew, for the first time, fear, and anger.

She dropped from the leaf to the ground below.

As the Hunter approached, Morgan struggled to get to his feet, but couldn't do it. On his hands and knees he waited for the end. The Hunter drew a long knife with a blade curved like a sickle, so black it was like a gash in the universe. He fingered it thoughtfully as he looked at Morgan. He spoke in a voice as cold as bones.

"I had hoped you would prove stronger, my son. You have disappointed me."

The Traveller appearing in the doorway of the hut ...

"All my life I have worked to escape my heritage

from you. I gave my life to the Light long ago."

The Hunter spat in contempt and moved slowly towards Morgan, owl-eyes unblinking. Morgan tried to find strength from somewhere to fend him off, but it was beyond him and the Hunter caught him by the hair and threw him to the ground on his back. He set one foot on Morgan's right arm to pin him there and knelt over him. For a few seconds they stared into each other's faces and Morgan could feel the Hunter's hot breath, then he looked down at the knife and poised it above Morgan's chest, ready to cut out his heart.

As Kate and David stood frozen with fear, a small figure darted past them, yelling "Get out! Get out!" and Ben was at the front door before they could stop him, bringing Gordon's second-best putter crashing down on the ghastly arm. There was a shriek and a noise like tearing cloth as it hit and the arm broke off and fell to the floor, turning back as it did so to a shower of dust and sifting down through the cracks between the floorboards.

Kate dragged Ben away from the door and together the three of them pushed the hall table against it to block the letterbox, then retreated to the bottom of the stairs.

Now the noise of attack came from all around them: blows to the roof and the shuttered windows and the walls, and most of all to the door. They could see it shaking. They clung to each other amid the buffeting noise and swirls of hot wind that rose from nowhere, waiting for the inevitable sound of splintering wood as Chaos broke down their world.

As the Hunter bent towards him, Morgan closed his eyes for the last time.

"Stop."

Neither the word nor the voice were loud, but they

filled everything. Even through his closed eyelids, Morgan could sense light of extraordinary intensity.

He heard the Hunter snarl and the pressure on his arm and chest was removed as he backed away.

A figure of flame and light stood near him, so impossibly bright that he could make nothing of it but a vaguely human shape. Before it the Lords cringed, hiding their eyes. The figure raised an arm and the Hunter's knife flew from his hand and burst into flame.

"Go," said the voice. **"You will not trouble these Worlds again. Your power here is ended. Go into the void."**

The Queen snarled. "If you battle us the power you release will blow the Worlds apart and Chaos will take them."

"You underestimate the power in me. I do not need to battle you, only to command you. Go!"

With a despairing shriek, the Lords of Chaos wavered and frayed and shattered like glass and were gone.

Kate, David and Ben clung together at the foot of the stairs, waiting for the end of the world they knew.

"I'm glad you're with me," shouted David. "It would have been terrible to be alone."

"Oh, David, it's all going, isn't it? Goodbye... Don't worry, Ben, it'll be over soon."

There was a noise so loud it was like silence and a shock wave threw them to the floor. The grandfather clock burst apart in a shower of wood and glass and metal, then there was silence.

As Morgan watched, his vision beginning to blur now, the brightness around the figure faded and it diminished and became Erda. She walked to where he lay and knelt down beside him, her eyes fixed on his.